DEATH IN

The First Màiri Maguire Cozy Mystery

KATE DARROCH

Astra Cozies

An imprint of Ad Astra Press Inc

STORIES
TO BRING A SPARKLE TO YOUR EYES

Ad Astra Press Inc

Darroch, Kate, author
Title: Death in Paris
Description: First edition I Ad Astra Cozies
Series: Màiri Maguire Cozy Mysteries; 1
Paperback ISBN: 978-1944690-04-5
Subjects: GSAFD: Mystery Fiction I Historical Fiction

Cover art by: Olena Levandovska

Release date: 30 March 2022

Ad Astra Press Inc.
8 The Green STE D
Dover, DE 19901

The Ilfracombe Centre
Devon EX34 9QB

https://AdAstraPress.co.uk
https://KateDarroch.com

Dedication Illustration is the interior of Kelvin Hall, Kelvinside, Glasgow, Scotland

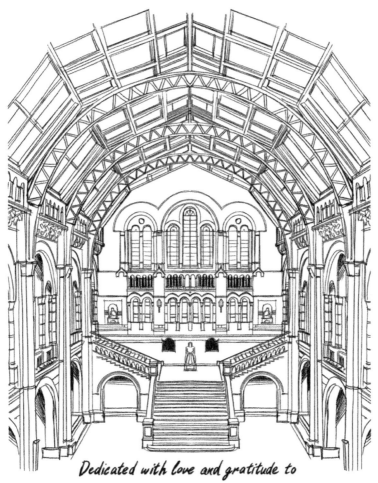

Dedicated with love and gratitude to
my darling Beta Readers
You Taught Me So Much! Thank You

CONTENTS

PROLOGUE

Up in the Air

Prologue

9:42 p.m. Sunday, 9th August, 1970

London Heathrow Airport, outside London, England, UK

News channel broadcasts relay through the airport's loudspeakers in the Arrivals lounge, shocking reports of the Peruvian Airlines LANSA Flight 502 exploding in mid-air, killing, according to the first news streaming in, anywhere between 91 and 99 people.

Not reassuring, Ferghal Reilly muses, seeing as how the very flight Magatte is on tonight may be a Lockheed Electra. KLM uses them, he knows. She is flying KLM. And her flight has been long delayed. But he isn't much worried. She leads a charmed life, does Magatte. How else would she have survived in the maelstrom of Italy's gun-running trade?

An incoming Jumbo Jet screams onto its runway.

Ferghal slumps in his padded seat in the waiting area, playing Cats Cradle because it keeps his hands limber. And because he likes weaving complex figures. He has just created a string shamrock, which (he thinks complacently) many would say is impossible. Nothing is impossible, he smiles to himself. Not for the man who is going to make a United Free Ireland the geo-political reality of some soon-to-come tomorrow.

But in fact Ferghal is wrong. At least about any danger of Magatte's plane exploding due to mechanical failure. KLM had stopped flying the design-flawed Lockheeds the year before.

Is he wrong about a United Free Ireland soon to come? Who knows? This is the time of The Troubles. Anything is possible.

That Magatte leads a charmed life is beyond dispute. She is forty five (although she looks younger) and Senegalese.

How did she become, way back in the '60s, a fixture in the Rome-centric gun-running trade?

Ferghal doesn't care. Is she carrying what he's waiting for? Nothing else matters to him. Certainly not the hundred lives lost in the Flight 502 crash. They weren't Irish lives.

A tall, dark woman walks into the Arrivals Hall, at the head of a swarm of weary and irritable travellers.

Ferghal rises to greet her.

The Summer Holidays

Chapter 1 The Summer Holidays

9:10 a.m. Friday, 17th July, 1970

Kelvin Academy for Girls, Kelvinside, Glasgow, Scotland, UK

The last day before the summer holidays. A tap on my Form 5A classroom door. The head girl peeps in. "Please, Miss Maguire. Mr McLaughlin's asking – can you take Form 5B too?" I nod; Deirdre files in with her classmates.

Other girls may have fallen victim to the current fashion for messiness, but Flower Power has not taken root in Kelvin Academy; the girls' faces shine, their hair is neat.

I'm proud of 5A and 5B, all set to burst into a vibrant classless society where a coal miner's daughter can get her degree just as easily as a debutante, and as easily as any man. I hope they'll enjoy their summer break as much as I'm going to enjoy mine.

First, though, there's the Teaching Appointments Fair this afternoon. I've promised to take the girls along to Kelvin Hall, where the foreign boarding schools are recruiting for their top drawer teaching appointments.

It will be nice for the girls to get an idea of the glamourous teaching jobs available abroad.

Glasgow-trained is still the first choice of all the best boarding schools, in spite of this stupid notion of "comprehensive" education. Not, of course, that a good school pays any attention to silly ideas like that. The one-size-fits-all education system is just another '70s fashion, a fad. Like micro-mini skirts and pop art, it will come and go.

I met a charming man at the Teaching Fair, Yasmin Yilmaz. Extremely good-looking, too. (Brian would have been jealous, I hope!) Professor Yilmaz is the headmaster of the Nautical High School in Istanbul. They need an English Studies department head. He insists I'm perfect for the job.

Flattering, but not my cup of tea. I like Glasgow just fine. Bad enough that Brian is away so much. Brian's a geologist. There's not a lot of live-in-your-hometown jobs for geologists.

Eleven years ago, when we graduated, he got a job with Geophysical Services International. So he's at sea most of the year, and his ship is usually near Singapore or Bali when they get shore leave. But he has six weeks home leave twice a year. We have a grand time then!

L uckily, it's only a short bus ride from Kelvin Hall to Merrylea, and pretty soon I'm strolling home from the bus stop. I can see Morag's wee red Mini sitting at the kerb. Great, she'll be baking already, if I know our Morag.

Katriona yields up her kitchen with a smile whenever Morag appears on our doorstep, for there's no-one else can cook like Morag, who is convinced Kat doesn't eat enough and Niall needs "feeding up". There's some mothers would bridle at that, but not our Kat.

It's true enough that when her man was taken so suddenly in that awful minehead disaster, Kat was beside herself with grief – glad of any helping hand, and tearfully grateful that I was there for her – but that was more than two years ago. Kat is eating fine now.

She'll have our tea ready to put on the table when I get in, and she doesn't need Morag to do the baking for her, not anymore. But only a nutter would say *No* to Morag's brandy snaps.

And if the price of Morag's cooking is that she fusses over her nephew more than any 10 year old much likes, not even Niall is daft enough to complain about that! He *is* very thin, but it's because he takes after his dad. Iain was dark and quiet, tall and thin, a complete contrast to Kat, who is small and plump (like all the Maguires) with fine milk-white skin and huge eyes.

It was something to see us in our teens, the four Maguire girls giving Exhibition Irish Dance in our plain green tunics that our mum had so carefully matched to the exact shade of our eyes, our upper bodies stock still, our auburn curls jigging. I never did understand how our bodies (plump even then) could be so still, and yet the curls dance as fast as our feet. But you could hear a pin drop when we began to dance, the four of us in a row.

Then Brenda emigrated to Canada, and after that Kat and Morag and me gave up the dancing. It just wasn't the same.

Pretty soon after, Morag settled down with Shuggie, who's been her sweetheart since the primary school playground, and then Kat married Iain after a lightning courtship, and I met Brian and he sailed off on a GSI ship.

I hope that Morag's man won't be with her today. Shuggie thinks all women should be happy to stay at home cooking, and I don't need him bringing my mood down in these precious first hours of the summer holidays.

Heading straight into the kitchen, I hug Morag. "Yummy! I smell brandy snaps." Just like I didn't know about the treat waiting for me the second I saw her car.

"Màiri!" she scolds fondly. "You'll get flour from my apron all over your good school dress! You're always so careless of your work clothes."

"Well, I've plenty of other good clothes, and all summer to wash them." I grin at her.

"Shuggie's working late." Morag is quick to excuse her man's absence. "I told him I wanted him to come celebrate the start of the school holidays with us, but you know what men are."

A great cook and a fond sister, our Morag, but tactful? Not so much.

The four of us sit down at the kitchen table to eat, and Niall is full of everything he's been doing with his mates.

S aturday morning and the first day of the holidays, double reason for a lie-in. But sunshine is pouring through my bedroom window, and we so seldom see the sun that I can't bring myself to waste the day.

Besides, I've promised to go shopping with my friend Lianna, who runs the bakery across the road from Kelvingrove Park, and has a rare Saturday off. A shame to waste a golden day like this in the Sauchiehall Street shops, but Lianna needs cheering up.

We'll get some lunch in Dino's café. Cappuccino and 'talie ice cream will be the very thing for her, if she hasn't started dieting again. Ever since she found out last winter that her soon-to-be-ex-husband Donal was cheating on her, Lianna has been dieting whenever she isn't bingeing on cream cakes and Barrs Irn Bru.

"I'm sooo fat" she moans. Lianna is not fat. She's dark and intense, very good-looking in a way that screams 'catch me *if* you can', for all that she's so prim and proper. But sometimes she squeezes herself into Hot Pants and hates how she looks in them. Nobody over 18 can look good in Hot Pants. You wouldn't catch me dead wearing them.

I'm happy Lianna has finally decided to have a makeover, but when I realised she'd chosen the first day of the summer hols, I could've killed her.

Never mind. Lianna and me have been pals since our first day at primary school together. Anything for a pal, right? I throw back the covers...

After a marathon shopping spree, we're eating spaghetti in one of the booths in Dino's and Lianna is telling me a long story about tax, which I can't understand.

She's being taxed as a business owner even though it's been months since she bowed out of the camping gear business she and Donal had been running together when she found out about him carrying on behind her back.

I know from painful experience that Lianna isn't going to be satisfied with me nodding and exclaiming "That's awful!" every five minutes. She wants me to understand all the ins and outs of her tale of woe, and she'll get really annoyed if I don't. So I try.

"I thought you did all the accounts for the business, Lianna?"

"That's right, Màiri. I did all the accounts when I was *there*. But I'm not there now, am I?"

I nod, hoping that will come across as sympathetic.

"In heaven's name, Màiri, at least *try* to understand, can't you? My charmer of an ex-husband – well, he'll be my ex soon, and it can't be soon enough! That nitwit Donal messed up the accounting records after I left, and he took all the money I'd put into a savings account for the taxes and spent it on some stupid souped-up car."

Now I'm interested. *How can a car cost a whole year's worth of a thriving business's taxes?* But I know better'n to ask, because Lianna would eat me alive.

"That's awful!" I really should have known better than to say that.

When she comes back down from orbit, Lianna tells me in baby words what happened. Donal has told the income tax people that she emptied the business bank account when she left him, and that he can't make sense of the mess she'd left the accounts in.

"And they *believe* him!"

I can help her with that.

"Do you have a name for the Inspector who's handling the case?"

"Yes, Charlie Stout."

"OK. What you do is, you make an appointment to see him, and you take your bank statements with you, and the last statements you have for the company's bank accounts, and you explain."

"Do you really think that will work?" Lianna looks doubtful, but that's an improvement on her looking furious.

"Of course it will!"

Well, how was I to know what would happen?

T o my amazement, the sunshine lasts for three whole weeks. I take Niall to the park, referee scratch football games, and come the first rainy day I'm sitting with Katriona in the teashop at the Art Gallery chatting about this and that while Niall tears around all over the museum.

"He's got to let off steam" explains his fond mum, and I certainly don't disagree. Besides, it's the Chinese exhibits that he's tearing around (we can see him through the glassed-in gallery or Kat would be down there with him; since Iain's death she never lets him out of her sight if she can possibly help it) and Niall is a bright wee laddie, so he'll be learning something about China without even knowing that he's doing it.

If Brian and I ever have a bairn, I hope the wee one will be as clever as Niall. I got a letter from Brian this morning, sent from Hong Kong. He'll be home in another few days, and he wants to take me to dinner at Rogano's his first night back!

I'm not getting any younger, and so I'm hoping that at last Brian is thinking of wedding bells.

When I see Lianna next, she's been to see Charlie Stout at the Kilmarnock Tax Office. I'd offered to go along with her, but she didn't want me.

Telling me about their interview afterwards, she's incandescent with rage. She says he had the nerve to try to flirt with her.

"Perhaps," I murmur soothingly, "he was just trying to set you at ease. Perhaps he's a little socially awkward."

Lianna sniffs, pitying my naivety. "No, he was flirting, well, trying to, the scunner."

I sigh. I hope she was less scathing when she was in his office. Men can get very upset when Lianna rejects them... and he *is* her tax inspector.

Wedding Bells

Chapter 2 Wedding Bells

9:40 p.m. Tuesday, 11th August, 1970

Rogano's Oyster Bar, Buchanan Street, Glasgow, Scotland, UK

And to think that I had *wanted* Brian to be thinking of wedding bells!

I'm reeling.

Twelve years with me, and now he's going to marry some bar girl he met on a five day shore leave in Singapore. "Mai-Lin is so sweet, so innocent." He's besotted. A *bar girl*, sweet and innocent!

"I wanted you to be the first to know, Màiri, because we've been such great friends, you and I, for so long. I hope that you and Mai-Lin will be friends too. I'm coming home for good now, you see. I got myself a teaching job at the Tech starting next term. It will be strange for Mai-Lin at first. But I know you'll help her to settle in."

This is too much. I can't bear it! As soon as he decides to marry this *floozy* he gets himself a job as a lecturer at Strathclyde University! Why couldn't he have done that long ago, and married me? We could have a Niall of our own by now.

And as if that isn't bad enough, he wants me to be her new best friend. To help her to settle in. I'll be a laughing stock. People will smile behind their hands if I pretend to like Brian's far eastern bride; they'll shake their heads pityingly if I don't. I'm "the woman scorned".

Oh, it's as much as I can do not to pick up the wine bottle and bop him over the head with it. But I don't.

"*Màiri, you're a lady.*" I remind myself. "*Ladies do not bop their ex-boyfriends over the head with wine bottles. Not in public.*"

But what am I to do? Next term is barely two weeks away. How can I show my face anywhere when Brian is strutting around all over Glasgow with Mai-Lin? Talk about a reddie!

And what's worse, he might even manage to nag me into playing the tourist guide to her...

And then, like a gift from God, I suddenly remember the job offer from Professor Yilmaz. I'm not going to take it, of course, but Brian doesn't know that. I'll take the wind right out of his sails, the cheeky sod.

"Sorry, Brian. I can't help you with that. I won't be here. I've been offered a job in Istanbul. Head of English Studies at a top school."

Brian's laughing so hard some wine goes down the wrong way. He isn't fooled for a second. "Oh, come *on*, Màiri," he wheezes between his gasps and coughs. "You don't really expect me to believe that a little homebody like you would ever take a job in Turkey! That's why things never got serious between us. You're so unadventurous. And me, I love adventure."

Never got serious! Twelve years, and it was never serious between us!

"No one could doubt you love adventure, Brian. Why, you're going to marry a *bar girl*. So who knows how many adventures are waiting for you, even here in Glasgow? But watching me introduce your exotic bride to her future *friends*" – oh, he kens fine what I mean – "won't be one of those adventures. I'll be in Istanbul when she arrives."

"Bit difficult to manage that, Màiri." He's still chortling. "She's up-stairs right now."

Oh! He's a pig. How could I ever have thought that I wanted to have his babies? He's a brute.

What am I going to *do*? I leave, of course. Instantly.

But as I stand outside Rogano's waiting for their doorman to find me a taxi, I wonder bleakly what I'll do tomorrow.

A s soon as I get home, I call Lianna. Just as I knew she would be, she's furious on my behalf.

"Let's get lunch at Dino's tomorrow, I'll call in sick at the bakery."

I'm too miserable to lecture her about how wrong it is for her to call in sick so that we can meet up. I want to sit eating ice cream with her and crying into my coffee – and right this minute her employer's superior claim on her time is not my first concern.

So we arrange to meet at noon, inside Dino's.

I sit crying and eating ice cream, and Lianna is brilliant. She keeps wiping the tears off my face with a nice soft clean hankie and ordering more ice cream, which she fetches herself from the counter so that I don't have to hide my red blotchy face from the waiter.

We're in a booth at the very back of the restaurant, and Lianna has pushed me into the seat with its high back to the door; no one except her can see me cry. So I cry and cry.

After a while, when Lianna comes back from the counter she isn't carrying ice cream, she's carrying two big brandy glasses. I'm not much of a drinker, and I'm feeling a bit sick from eating so much ice cream. Brandy has no appeal for me. Throwing myself into the Clyde has a lot of appeal for me.

"Drink it. You need some backbone put into you. You've got to help me plan."

"What do you mean, plan? There's nothing *to* plan. I'm a laughing stock."

Grimly. "Oh yes there is. That gobshite— "

"Lee*ana*!"

"Well, he is!"

"Lianna, we're in public. Someone might hear you. No matter what Brian's done"

"Who's talking about Brian? That g—*pig* Charlie Stout has sent me a tax demand for more money than the house my mother left me is worth. *And* penalties! I'm barely making eating money at the bakery. Donal has run through all the tax money. The divorce costs ate up all my savings. And now that filthy *animal* of a tax fiend has the unspeakable nerve to say to me: 'We can do nothing about the tax demand, my dear. You've spent the company's tax money and must make that good, but perhaps something could be done about the fines and penalties *if you're nice to me, my dear.*'"

"Oh, Lianna." Suddenly my own worries look pretty small.

Lianna swigs her brandy moodily.

"I'd like to wring that man's neck. D'ye think he'll come to his senses if my brothers give him a doin'?"

But despite the hope in her voice, Lianna must know her brothers can't give Stout a doing, richly though he deserves it. All five Stuart boys are fine figures of men, over 6 foot tall and champions at the caber throwing. But they can't lay a finger on Stout without getting locked up in the pokey. The law takes a dim view of assault on Her Majesty's servants.

An idea takes slow shape in my mind.

"Lianna, your brothers are fine strapping men, aye, and could throw yon Stout across the room as soon as look at him. But I'm thinking maybe they shouldnae do that, not at all, at all.

Maybe what they want to do is, they just talk to him quiet like about how upset you are, and how much it upsets them to see you upset...   p'rhaps they'll bend a horseshoe at him, which they can explain to him they'd brought along for luck."

I tap my fingers on the table in a dirge – Dah Dah Dah Da Da Dah

"And if you were away for a bit? Maybe they might turn up other places than his office, all sorrowful, greetin' over how much they miss you... and how feart they are that you'll do yourself a mischief, and all through the worry over your taxes."

I decide to take a sip of the brandy.

"But never a bit of harm they'll do him, and they'll be sure to take recordings of everything they say to him, in case the poliss should come at them..." Another small sip.

"How long do you think he could stand that, Lianna? Three months? Four? Your brothers are awfully big men."

"What's in your mind, Màiri?"

"I'm thinking I've got a job offered me in Istanbul, and a Head who would let me choose my own assistant – and who'd know you'd gone there, Lianna?"

Well, we talk about it a bit more, and then Gino, whose turn it is to manage the café today (all Dino's sons take a turn at the management) lets me use their telephone to place a collect call to the Nautical High School. I get hold of Professor Yilmaz easy enough.

"Miss Maguire! How good to hear from you. Does this mean that you will be coming to us?"

"Well, professor, I was thinking... You did say I'd have my own assistant to handle all the paperwork for my department?"

"Of course. Of course. Every department head has an assistant for paperwork."

"Well, you see, it would be kind of strange for me at first, alone in a faraway place, and so I was hoping..."

"Yes, dear lady? Yes? You were hoping?"

"I can choose my own assistant?"

"Naturally. Yes. We discussed this. You choose."

"Well, I have a friend here in Glasgow, she has an excellent head for paperwork and figurework and all that kind of thing..."

"And you wish her to come here with you? Of course. There is a little set of rooms, two bedrooms, a sitting room, a bathroom, perfect for two ladies to share."

So that was all right. We got it all sorted on the spot, the professor being extremely courteous about all the arrangements. There's a very generous relocation package. Professor Yilmaz says Lianna can have relocation expenses too, although strictly speaking an assistant isn't entitled to expenses. That's good of him. I can tell I'm going to be well treated at his school.

"I shall be charmed, Miss Maguire, to meet this paragon of a lady whom you have chosen to assist you."

Lianna and I walk three shops down Sauchiehall Street to the Thomas Cook shopfront, the travel agents, to book passage to Istanbul in ten days time. While we're there and the Thomas Cook lassie is on the phone sorting out our passage across Europe on the train, she shows us a brochure for City Breaks.

These City Breaks are a package holiday tour. You can go to London or Paris or Amsterdam. It's very good value. Whilst she's holding on the phone, the lassie is busy talking to us about how great it will be if we have a City Break holiday before we start our journey to Istanbul.

And right away I see the big advantage; I'd be gone from Glasgow before anyone knows anything about Brian's beastly bar girl. I can hold my head up leaving. And before I get back, everyone will be all talked out over Brian's weird life choices. I won't have to pretend not to notice that I'm being laughed at, or even worse, pitied.

We choose Paris, which is pretty ironic. But Lianna is having fun for the first time in the last eight months. "Who needs men to visit the City of Romance?" She winks. "Who needs men, full stop! We can have an exciting adventure on our own."

And Paris is where the Express train to Istanbul starts off from, so that's good.

I'm just as glad that Lianna fancies Paris. What with The Troubles, and IRA activity flaring up, and me being Irish, I'm thinking that maybe London isn't the best place to be staying for long. We don't want to have the poliss there taking it into their heads that we've come from Belfast instead of Glasgow and are plotting some kind of devilment.

Lianna says I'm daft even to think of a thing like that.

After we get some French francs and a lot of Travellers Cheques at Thomas Cook's – they have a Bureau de Change right there in their shop, very convenient – Lianna and me part company, because we have to let our families know what we're doing.

Naturally, Lianna has the more difficult job, briefing her brothers, but I envy her.

Because telling Kat is going to be fraught. And also I have to resign from the academy, which means letting Aloysius McLaughlin know right away, because it would be a rotten thing to do to him, letting him start the new term all unsuspecting, and I won't do that.

Aloysius McLaughlin and I have always had a good working relationship; he doesn't deserve that kind of poke in the nose. And besides, I want a reference from him.

I'm freshly engulfed in annoyance and misery at the thought of Brian's bizarre behaviour. How could he do this to me? OK, so he's met someone new. He could have been a gentleman about it. He could have written the news to me, given me time to prepare.

Just look what's happening instead! The disruption to my life, my family, and – I hadn't thought of it until now – my colleagues, my girls.

It's going to be very inconvenient for Aloysius, finding a replacement only two weeks before term begins – and me not even there to do a smooth handover.

My poor girls. Yes, 5A and 5B are happily finding their way in the exciting world of New Wave Seventies Britain's classless society, but what about 4A and 4B, who will be this September's 5A and 5B?

They're expecting me to guide them through the minefield of the New Curriculum and into the safe harbour of Glasgow University.

So instead, they come back from the summer break, and no Miss Maguire. Maybe Aloysius will have to bring in a substitute who won't know the girls, who won't be in tune with our school's way of doing things, who might even be in favour of comprehensive education.

At the thought of my poor girls sitting there all bewildered, I furtively wipe away a few tears. "*What's come over you, Màiri Maguire?*" I chide myself. "*Greetin' in the street...*"

I'm getting worried now, because you never know, this Istanbul thing might not work out...

How to resign is a bit of a difficulty, because the school has closed down for its semi-annual two-week-long "spring cleaning". And the McLaughlin family is not on the phone.

Luckily, they live only two streets away from us, right beside the church. I decide I'll walk round there now, and tell Aloysius first off. Get it over with.

T hat was hard enough, but it's nothing to telling our Kat. My poor big sister is so bewildered and worried for me that eventually I have to tell her about Brian (Lianna's tussle with the taxman I keep to myself).

Then it's worse, because she's crying at the thought of me losing my man *and* leaving her; and I know that inside she's keening for poor Iain all over again. I feel like a monster.

But now she's rushing over to me, my brave loyal Katriona, and she hugs me, sobbing out against my neck. "You're better off without him! Oh, far better off! You'll have a grand time in Turkey, and come home with a gorgeous Turk on your arm, and bad cess to him, the stupid gal-loot, he doesn't know when he's well off. I never did like him." (Kat adores Brian, and oh! the patter they spark off each other...) "My poor Màiri" – she gulps in some air – "you'll have a super time in Istanbul, they tell me the weather's just lovely there. To think of us all freezing in the rain here, and you cozy warm, and treated like a queen. They tell me those Turkish men are so charming and attentive. I'll just go and put the kettle on." She retreats to the kitchen, to have her cry out in peace.

Niall comes in just then, and I tell him that I'll be off to Paris in the morning and then on to Istanbul. The thought of a resident auntie's departure from his life does not faze him a bit.

"Cool! Bring me back a working model of the Eiffel Tower, will you, Auntie Màiri? And one of a mosque!"

It's always construction toys he wants... he'll be an engineer, like his father... poor Kat.

'Tis better to
Travel hopefully...

Chapter 3 'Tis Better to Travel Hopefully...

9:30 a.m. Thursday, 13th August, 1970

Glasgow Central Station, Gordon Street, Glasgow, Scotland, UK

Next day me and Lianna meet up at Central Station, all excited, and we're off to London. Thomas Cook have booked us into a nice quiet Bed & Breakfast place in Bayswater. We'll have dinner in a good restaurant and see a play. I fancy *The Mousetrap*. It's been running for years and years, so it must be prime. And I do like a bit of a mystery.

We'll be going down to Southampton the following morning by the boat train, and then the ferry to Le Havre, and lunch – the famous French cooking! And then on to Paris. Seven nights in a nice *pension* – that's the French word for small hotel – and then we travel overland to Istanbul, on the train, which will be a big adventure in itself.

We've booked a two-berth compartment, Second Class. The train staff change it into a sitting room during the day, it all sounds very exciting.

I did wonder if I should splurge on First Class for us, but it was awfully dear. And in Thomas Cook's they showed us a diagram so we could see our little compartment would be absolutely private. And going by the pictures, it looked pretty luxurious too.

I did book First Class in England, though, remembering what it was like the last time I went down to London - crammed in with seven other people in a tiny Second Class carriage.

As we're getting onto the train, Lianna says she's sure she caught a glimpse of Charlie Stout. I tell her severely not to let her nerves run away with her.

We have a lovely lunch in the First Class dining compartment, and when we go to our seats after lunch, by pure luck we have a carriage all to ourselves. There might have been another four people in there, but there aren't.

By the time we've settled in at our B&B place in Bayswater, we're in a bit of a rush to get to the theatre. But luckily, they do a knife-and-fork tea where we're staying, so that's all right.

It turns out to be rather an adventure just getting to The Ambassadors Theatre. The Tube, London's subway system, is difficult to make sense of because London has lots and lots of underground train lines, all different, not like in Glasgow, where we have just the one subway train track going around in a giant circle.

We get to the theatre in good time, only we can't get Stalls seats. That's a surprise; we'd thought that there would be plenty of seats on a Thursday night – it's the day before Payday, after all. They offer us Balcony seats instead.

That upsets Lianna, she's afraid of heights. She doesn't want to go up to the Balcony seats. I manage to persuade her, but she's shuddering by the time we take our seats in the front row.

And then, if you please, she says Charlie Stout is sitting in the middle of the Stalls, next to a stout grey-haired woman in a yellow dress.

"Where?" I lean forward just as the lights go out and the curtain goes up.

We both enjoy the play very much. Agatha Christie is such a clever writer. And the beds at our B&B are comfy. Next morning they give us a good cooked breakfast, on the Menu it says it's an Irish Breakfast. I don't quite like to ask what the difference is between an Irish breakfast and an English breakfast, because I'm not all that keen on Irish jokes, and you never know, the answer may be a joke.

Major Ellis Peverel is across town in Whitehall, enjoying an English breakfast which no one in government would dream of comparing to an Irish breakfast, although the difference is in fact very slight.

An Irish breakfast is an English breakfast (bacon, eggs, sausages, tomatoes, a fried slice of bread, fried potatoes, and mushrooms, eaten with toast and marmalade) all except for toast, instead of which there's soda bread – or wheaten bread – and fried potato scones instead of the fried slice. Màiri needn't have worried, there was no Irish joke.

The Major doesn't consider anything connected with the Irish to be a joke. As the highest ranking English official in the new international anti-terrorist initiative ATJF (anti-terrorist joint forces), he regards the IRA as a dangerous criminal nuisance and otherwise never thinks of the Irish at all.

What Major Peverel thinks about night and day is getting Britain's ATJF accord with France and Italy running like clockwork. And so in an effort to fortify the accord by renewing his bonds with the leaders of the wartime French Resistance, almost all of whom are now highly placed in French governmental circles, the Major is travelling to Paris today.

Glancing at his watch, Ellis abandons his breakfast half-eaten. There is barely enough time to comb his moustache and change out of his Saville Row suit into a dress uniform before the Ministry chauffeur arrives to drive him to the boat train.

Harry Brown is the only one enjoying his breakfast to the full without any qualms about jokes or any thoughts of stern duty. Mr Brown is not in the habit of allowing intellectual activity of any kind to interfere with his enjoyment of his food, but this morning he needs to take in hand that stupid Irish git, Ferghal Reilly.

Not until he has finished his double soss with extra slice, though. Mopping up the last runnel of egg yolk with a corner of toast, Harry pushes his plate aside, lights a Benson & Hedges, and takes a gulp of the brick-orange liquid that the lorry drivers who breakfast here call tea.

There's an excellent view of the Le Havre dock and the Channel water beyond through the café's plate-glass window, which is why Harry chose this eatery as Ferghal's lookout spot.

Settling back comfortably (for there is no knowing how long this conversation may go on) he checks once more that Ferghal's chair is facing the window squarely, and begins.

"You don't know Magatte."

"Ah, I do so, boss," the numbskull prattles. "I met her at London airport a couple of weeks ago, do you not mind that?"

Restraining with little difficulty an impulse to silence Ferghal with a punch – a true leader is always calm – Harry asks calmly,

"Ferghal, what did I tell you about contradicting me?"

"Sorry, boss."

"You're not likely to get near enough Magatte to speak to her, but if you do, you don't."

Ferghal opens his mouth, but catching sight of the boss's glittering eye, closes it again.

"Who do you speak to, Ferghal?"

"The woman whose luggage Magatte points out."

"She won't point out the luggage, Ferghal, she'll point out the woman."

"Yes, but how can she point anything out to me if I'm not to go near her?"

"We talked about this, Ferghal. When the ferry is coming in, you'll be watching through the window here."

"Yes, boss."

"And you'll see Magatte talking to a woman."

"Yes, boss."

"The woman she talks to is the one you're to get into conversation with on the train."

"What if she talks to more than one woman?"

"She won't."

"She might."

This is why Harry Brown had decided to begin rehearsing Ferghal so early in the day, hours before he needs to go into action...

"Ferghal, what did I tell you about contradicting me?"

"Sorry, boss."

Me and Lianna splurge on a taxi to take us to the boat train, where we're booked into First Class, and on the way down to Southampton, Lianna doesn't see any phantom Charlie Stouts.

We're both pretty excited boarding the ferry, now we're really on our way to Paris, because the ferry journey is partly in France (well, on French water, the boundary line between England and France is halfway across the English Channel).

As we're going down the stairs, or gangway, or whatever they call it, on our way towards the refreshment saloon, suddenly Lianna sees Charlie Stout again. She claims he's at the bar, by himself. I look. There's no one at the bar. I point that out to Lianna. I tell her she's getting to be obsessed with Charlie Stout.

But she just gets that mulish look she sometimes gets, so we go back up onto the deck. It's nice on deck. There's a lovely breeze, and the view of the sea is lovely too.

The travellers' luggage is all piled up on deck, so I go and perch on the bigger of my two suitcases and it makes quite a good seat. Lianna perches beside me, on my other suitcase.

Lianna has far fancier luggage than me, a matched set. A smart little travelling case and three bigger suitcases, all in nice graduated sizes, very posh. My suitcases are all scuffed up.

After a bit, I go down to the saloon to bring us up cups of tea; the travel people said it would be the last chance for a decent cup of tea until we're in our own quarters in Istanbul and we can brew it ourselves.

So we perch there on my suitcases sipping our tea and we're having just the grandest time!

As the shoreline grows closer, people begin trickling up onto the deck from the refreshment saloon. I see a tall, dark woman bundled up in a windbreaker admiring Lianna's luggage set. People are always admiring Lianna's clothes and things; she has such excellent taste.

The woman comes over to Lianna and me, and we all fall into conversation. She's got a strong accent, I can't quite place it, it doesn't sound French.

But when I ask her if she'll be travelling to Paris on the train like us, she says that she won't be travelling on because she lives in Le Havre. Then she says what a beautiful day it is, with the breeze just right. Lianna and me are dead chuffed that we've got such perfect weather.

We all chat for another few minutes. Most people are clustered near the gangway off the boat, a bit silly really, where's the rush? The woman drifts off and Lianna and I have that side of the deck all to ourselves again, which is nice.

I'm so full that I'm waddling! French cooking certainly lives up to its reputation! Our lunch at Le Havre was incredible. I had three helpings of the chocolate mousse. As I glance down at my tummy, wondering if maybe from being so full of mousse it's grown a little bit bigger, Lianna grabs my arm. "Quick, Màiri, look now!" she squeaks out.

I look up quickly, but I can't see anything out of the ordinary, just a lot of people milling about, which is what you'd expect because we're heading for our train to Paris.

"What?" Her nails are biting into my arm. Really, Lianna has been in a very funny mood ever since we started our journey. She looks down into my face (Lianna is about 4 inches taller than me) and whatever she sees there she doesn't seem to like, for she glances up and out, and as she does, her nails bite even deeper into my arm.

"It's too late."

All the sorrow in the world weighs down her voice.

"He's gone now."

I don't ask who "he" is, because I'm afraid that the answer will be "Charlie Stout".

We've reached our train and climb aboard.

The train isn't too packed, and after that marvellous lunch I'm feeling mellow, so I'm quite happy just to sit in the rail carriage, half-reading, half-dozing. But habit is strong, and by half-past four, I want my tea. I ask Lianna whether we'd rather take the risk of paying for tea that turns out to be undrinkable, or do without our tea altogether.

In the end, we go into the dining carriage for afternoon tea, because the French don't do a proper knife-and-fork tea. But Lianna's broad-minded and so am I. We have no objection to eating cream cakes at teatime.

Coming into the dining carriage, we pass a table where an elderly English military man sits alone, glancing through a small leather notebook, a cane resting slantwise on his tabletop – his tea has not yet been served. I'm surprised to see he's in uniform, he looks as if he's past compulsory retirement age, an ancient relict.

Lianna spots a woman who lives near her, Aileen McPherson, so we join her at her table.

Aileen is travelling with Senga MacAuliffe, a friend of hers whom we don't know because she lives in the Highlands. With them is an exquisite little lady, very chic, with laughing black eyes, who introduces herself as Valerie Garnier, tour guide for their package holiday, which turns out to be the self-same package that we're on. What luck! Now we can get the low-down on Paris whilst eating cream cakes, an excellent combination.

As we're all saying *Hello*, we're joined by someone Valerie knows, Ferghal Reilly. Despite his name, Ferghal lives and works in Paris. He's an art dealer, and for sure that man has kissed the Blarney Stone. Oh, the Black Irish good looks of him! And does the man know it? Full of himself, he is.

Ferghal tells us that he does quite well for himself by importing paintings from Scotland, Ireland, and occasionally the Bayswater Road in London, where it seems that despite all the splashed-paint-on-black-velvet "artworks", now and then a true artist is driven to exhibit on the park railings by the need to put food on the table.

Whilst Ferghal is holding forth, I glance around the dining carriage. Two men seated alone together at a table quite near us are holding hands. That's sweet – and it's all thanks to our recent Prime Minister, Harold Wilson (of course he wasn't the Prime Minister at the time) for it was his reforms that meant British men can now hold hands in public without fear of being banged up in the pokey – and these two are British, I feel sure. One looks Welsh, and there's something about the other puts me in mind of Carnaby Street.

A few tables are empty, and at the other end of the carriage a businessman sits surrounded by papers and charts, his teacup pushed to the side, one hand holding a piece of paper up to his piggy little eyes, the other pushing half a buttered muffin into his fat-lipped mouth.

A train attendant is delivering the military man's tea service, and a stout grey-haired woman with a pleasant face edges past him as she comes in. She walks up to our table, but seeing that it's full, she slides into the seat of the empty table across the way.

Valerie smiles at her and starts to make an introduction, and Ferghal courteously moves over to her table so that she doesn't have to sit alone. I'm pleased he did that, maybe he isn't quite as full of himself as he seems.

Her eye caught by Ferghal's movement, Lianna begins to turn towards the newly seated lady, ready to acknowledge the introduction which any moment now Valerie will effect...

...just as a nondescript little man enters the carriage and the military man at the table by the entrance goes ballistic!

Seizing his cane with a wordless roar, he brandishes it like a weapon (despite very obviously needing it to steady a gimpy leg) over-balancing his hot water jug as his other hand grabs at his tabletop to haul himself onto his feet. His dishes all go flying.

He has managed to jump up – only his fury lending him the ability to stand without falling – and attempts to bring his cane down hard on the little man's head.

The little man dodges away from the blow, but he can't get past the roaring lunatic, who is shouting at him with tremendous passion, thrashing about him with his cane in the most astonishing surge of violent energy, even though he can hardly stay upright and looks as if he'll fall any second.

"You damned scoundrel! You double-dyed liar! You little sneak! You embezzling skunk! I'll skin you alive! I'll break this cane over your lying skull, see if I don't!"

And with another startling lunge, he actually manages to connect his cane with the little man's shoulder, quite a vicious blow.

The little man screams. Lianna screams. The attacker is still roaring. And over it all, in sweet measured tones as penetrating as any sergeant-major's on the parade ground "Charlie, what have you done now?" blares out the Glasgow-accented voice of the grey-haired woman.

I see it all in a flash. I'm not going to get any cream cakes, and bringing Lianna to Paris has been a mistake.

But I'm giving myself too much credit. I don't yet know the full dimensions of this fiasco, because it happens that I'm sitting by the window, and Lianna's seat gives onto the central passageway. As she rises, shaking, there is nothing to prevent her from moving anywhere she likes – and I don't even want to think about what Lianna might like to do to Charlie Stout.

Ferghal looks from my agonised expression to Lianna's contorted face, and proves himself a man of action. He moves smoothly into the passage just behind Lianna and catches at her arms. "Wheesht" he murmurs. "Sure I think they'll get on better without a lady in the mix."

Lianna's last vestige of control slips. The hated enemy is in front of her, and she is going to get him where it hurts, even if that means hurting someone else first.

Forgetting for a moment that she is a lady, Lianna elbows Ferghal viciously (I really can't bring myself to say where) and screams "Let me at him."

Ferghal, to his credit, somehow manages to absorb the blow and stay on his feet, and he hasn't let go of Lianna. In fact, he tightens his grip.

Lianna is beside herself, screaming at poor Ferghal. "Let me at him! I'll strangle him! I'll cut his lying tongue out and stuff it down his throat! I'll kill him! I'll break every bone in his rotten body! I'll throttle him!"

Obviously she can't cut his tongue out (there are no sharp enough knives in the carriage) but I wouldn't wager a groat on the chances of her not doing the rest.

Not while Ferghal has a good hold of her though, and he's certainly not loosening his grip.

The lunatic by the entranceway has Stout trapped; he can't get out and he can't get past. And even although Stout is leaping about nimbly, and the military relict can hardly stand, every now and then a vicious blow from the cane connects.

The military gentleman is still roaring insults and threats. Stout screams every time the cane hits him. Lianna never stops screaming about how she's going to strangle Stout and/or break him to bits (her precise intention isn't fully clear, though not from want of poor Lianna trying to make her wishes known). Ferghal is still murmuring soothingly to her. He might as well save his breath.

The noise level is indescribable.

It's almost as bad as when 3C first pour out into the playground after double period maths.

Recognising that cream cakes are out of the question, I pour myself a cup of tea. It's just as undrinkable as Thomas Cook had warned us it would be.

Eventually everything calms down. Stout manages to escape from the dining carriage. The military gentleman collapses back into his seat. He is taking a reviving nip from a flask.

When his collapse left the entranceway available, Mrs Stout calmly followed her husband, appearing quite incurious as to why a decrepit elderly Englishman and a perfectly normal looking Scotswoman are both after his blood.

I expect that she's used to it, the taxman is never a popular figure.

Lianna has sunk back into her seat, put her head down on the tea table and is quietly weeping. Ferghal is trying to soothe her. I have misjudged the man. Clearly, when the chips are down, he has community spirit enough.

It's a miracle that the train attendants didn't stop the train and send for the police; but I expect that the French, who are very excitable, have a more tolerant attitude towards this kind of argy-bargy than most other nations.

Being Scots Irish, I take it in my stride; you see worse in Buchanan Street every Saturday night when the pubs come out. Glasgow is a warm friendly city, with fine architecture and a great music scene, but it's no place for them as faint at the sight of blood.

And as for the Irish who live in Glasgow, our men are poets and dreamers (we women have to be very practical) but anybody who thinks that a poet can't fight with the best of 'em is just begging for a bloody nose.

The train attendants won't come into the carriage, I expect that they're off having a good gossip somewhere, but I suppose they might be afraid that another fight will break out.

So I'm a wee bit annoyed that I can't get my tea, but not bothered otherwise. Ferghal, of course, being Irish, thinks nothing at all of Lianna's outburst.

To my surprise, Valerie's eyes are twinkling. She seems to have enjoyed the uproar. Aileen is politely pretending that it didn't happen, and her friend Senga takes her cue from Aileen.

O ur train pulls into the Gare du Nord at the scheduled arrival time of 8:16 p.m. Dusk is just closing in. The Eiffel Tower is all lit up and it looks stunning. By now over her fury at Stout, Lianna is entranced, and loudly admires the Tower. This doesn't surprise me at all, for Lianna is a creature of moods.

Valerie tells us that our package tour is booked into the Hôtel Albert in the Rue du Faubourg Saint-Denis, too close to the station for it to be worthwhile queuing up for taxis. But it turns out that getting from the station to our *pension* is a pretty tiring walk when you're struggling through the unknown and crowded streets of Paris with your luggage.

Everyone who's on the tour straggles through the doors of the Hôtel Albert in a tired clump. It's hard to manoeuvre our luggage into the small revolving door partitions; we have to go in one person at a time and push hard on the glass part.

Then we queue up to check in, which seems to take an inordinately long time. But this looks like a nice place, even if the service at reception is awfully slow.

Ferghal is long gone off to his home, lucky him. Major Peverel (after a few reviving nips the relict had stumped over to introduce himself and to apologise, in a very gentlemanly way, for "making a row") is staying at a different hotel. I hope it's as nice as this one.

E llis Peverel has gone straight from Gare du Nord to the British Embassy, and is just in time to join the end of the receiving line.

He congratulates himself silently on efficient use of time; only one day spent travelling, and that begun with a briefing at Whitehall and ending at a reception in Paris where most of his old chums from the war days are gathered. A top hole way to enlist support for his joint task forces op.

He'd lucked in at Le Havre too; been on the train when that bad hat Harry Brown joined it. Clear as daylight Brown must have been there to keep his eye on a new stooge. Perhaps that too-good-looking Irishman. Or the little tour guide.

Whatever Brown is plotting, the Sûreté will want to put a stop to it; and now ATJF can serve Brown up to them on a silver platter. A good omen for British-French accord.

And then that slimy embezzling blackmailer whats-his-name had turned up. The Major has never had more fun improvising an excuse to introduce himself to an asset. One of those four women was Brown's target, that's obvious. Not clear which one yet, but they're all staying at the same hotel, so it's easy enough to track them…

He soon spots one of his closest associates in the Resistance days. It is astonishing how little the man has changed. A little thinner, a little greyer – a little more exhausted.

We were all tired enough during the guerrilla days, thinks Peverel, but the poor old boy looks as if he hasn't slept for a year.

"Ah, mon vieux" – Peverel is accosted seconds later – "what a pleasure it is to see you again. But you look as though you have not slept for a year. Are they working you so hard at ATJF?"

"Pretty hard, old boy. And the responsibility of top command gets to you. You'd know all about that, of course. You've been heading up Direction générale de la sécurité extérieure for quite a while now, haven't you?" His comrade nods. "A little tidbit for you. Bad hat from a decade ago is on your turf. He'll bear close watching."

"Ah" murmurs the Frenchman, never one to waste words.

"Happened to spot him on the train from Le Havre." Peverel continues. "Had a bit of luck, old man. Another villain was on the train. I collared him years ago, but he got off." He grins.

"Had some fun with that. Thrashed the blighter. Then scraped an introduction to Brown's target by apologising for making a scene. Could have been any one of four women, so I had to do something pretty spectacular to get noticed."

Both men laugh, it's the kind of joke old soldiers relish...

M e and Lianna have been in the queue about ten minutes when Lianna says she's going to powder her nose. She looks like a wraith. Although I'm tired too, I can see that she needs a seat pretty badly.

So I say, "OK. I can check us in. Why not take a seat in the lobby after you've been to the Ladies, and wait for me? No need for the both of us to stay on our feet."

She flashes me a grateful smile, and although she's tired to death, I can see that my own dear Lianna is back. She's herself again, the craziness on the train just a memory.

Charlie Stout is playing least-in-sight, very wise of him. Aileen and her friend, who were first in the queue, have completed check-in and gone up to their room. Valerie has disappeared; and to my surprise and embarrassment, I find Mrs Stout standing behind me in the queue.

The least I can do is apologise, and so we get into conversation.

Mrs Stout tells me that "my Charlie" had been so little affected by the beating he took in the train that he's off playing the tourist. "He just couldn't wait to go up to the top of the Eiffel Tower," Mrs Stout says in her placid way. "I told him it would still be there tomorrow, but he only laughed and went off, leaving me behind to check us in and see to the luggage. Ah, well! They're all little boys at heart, aren't they?"

I'm relieved that Mrs Stout is inclined to be friendly, and far too tired to care whether her husband is at the Eiffel Tower or drinking in some nightclub, which seems to be a more likely destination for a man like him.

At last, I arrive at the head of the slow-moving queue, and the hotel people want to see my passport, so I take it out of my bag to show them and to my surprise, they don't give it back. "Regulations, madame, the *passeport* go in the hotel safe. The gendarmes, they come to inspect the *passeports*, and we keep the *cartes* safe for you." Oh well, when in Rome...

Continuing with the check-in, the hotel staff find that Lianna is sharing the room, and then they refuse to give me our keys until her passport is handed over too. I look around the lobby, but I can't see her.

I have had enough of this. It's nearly half-past nine by now. I'm tired, I didn't have my tea, and if I don't get checked in soon, I won't get any dinner either, because I am not going out to explore a strange city without a meal inside me and the hotel's dining room stops taking dinner orders at 9:45 p.m. sharp.

I stiffen, and give the tiresome clerk the look I give girls whom I catch talking in class.

"Miss Stuart will give you her passport when she comes to collect her room key. Meanwhile, you will have our luggage put in our room, and you will give me my room key now. I'm going to get something to eat. When you see Miss Stuart, please tell her I'm ordering dinner for us both."

I hold out my hand. Looking a bit unhappy, the clerk turns to get my room key from the keyboard behind him and puts a huge brass key fob on my palm. "Room 101, madame."

So I go into the dining room and ask for the menu, which they call a *carte*. The waiter pours water for me while he waits for me to choose our food, and I begin to feel a little less cross. "Two steaks with *pommes frites, s'il vous plait. Crème glacée.* No wine."

As I'm handing back the *carte,* Mrs Stout comes up to my table. The hands of the dining room clock are standing at 9:43. She hastily lays her hand on the waiter's arm.

"I'll have whatever this lady is having." With that, she turns back to me, smiling. "Well, I got here just in time! Another minute and I'd have gone dinnerless, eh?"

She lays her hand on the back of the chair across from me. "Since we're both alone, shall we eat together?" Politely, she is waiting for me to say *Yes* before pulling the chair out.

"Well, actually, I'm waiting for my friend Lianna. I expect she'll be here any minute." Mrs Stout takes her hand off the chair. "But of course we'd be happy for you to join us, er, that is, if you don't mind that, that, uuum, well, that my friend doesn't like your husband."

Mrs Stout laughs and seats herself. "She's in good company."

We chat of this and that and Mrs Stout tells me to call her Yvonne. Another ten minutes has gone by and there's still no sign of Lianna. I wonder if she's stuck in a futile argument with the hotel clerk about handing over her passport.

I give Yvonne an apologetic smile. "I can't think what's keeping Lianna. Maybe I'd better go and look for her." A tiny frown creases the space between Yvonne's eyebrows. "Yes, it has been quite a while since she went off to powder her nose – perhaps we should go look."

I'm startled, but then I remember, she'd been behind us in the queue. Of course she heard me talking to Lianna. She rises. What can I do?

We go together to find Lianna, pausing only to tell the Maître d' at the restaurant entrance that we'll soon be back.

But we aren't back soon. Lianna isn't arguing with the clerk at the reception desk. She isn't sitting in the lobby. She isn't in the powder room. We ask the reception clerk and the bellboy and the powder room attendant if they've seen her, but they haven't.

I go up to our room, to see if she's there, noticing as I let myself in that my brass key fob is engraved 101. Lianna isn't in our room.

Feeling foolish, I check the Ladies Room on this floor. But Lianna isn't there either.

Where can she be? I am beginning to get just a little worried...

Yvonne has checked the lobby again whilst I was in the room, and popped out to see whether Lianna had felt the need of a breath of air. But there's absolutely no sign of her.

Reluctantly, I decide that we'd better ask for the hotel manager's help, and so I ask the clerk at reception to fetch him. The clerk explains that they're short-staffed; the manager is filling in for the bartender.

We turn to the bar, and as we go in, I hear Lianna's distinctive laugh. Once again, she has temporarily forgotten that she is a lady, and is sitting at the bar letting some Frenchman buy her drinks.

I lose no time in reclaiming her, withering the hopeful Frenchman with a killing look, and the three of us go in to eat.

I do my best to ignore the hurt looks that the waiter casts me as he serves the meal. It has been kept warm for us too long and is by now over-cooked. It's clear that it wounds his pride to serve a less than perfect meal.

Yvonne doesn't seem to mind that her meal has been spoilt by Lianna's ill-timed sociability. That's one very calm lady; nothing appears to ruffle her placidity.

The ice cream isn't as good as Dino's. It's not proper 'talie ice cream at all. Huh! So much for the wonderful French cooking.

Crime
Passionel?

Chapter 4 Crime Passionnel?

7:50 a.m. Saturday, 15th August, 1970

Hôtel Albert, Rue du Faubourg Saint-Denis, Paris, France

I'm relieved to see, next morning, that Lianna is fresh as a daisy, no sign of a hangover. We go down to breakfast nice and early.

The lobby holds a small crowd of gendarmes; I expect that they've come to have a look at our passports as we've been told is the French custom. Odd that they seem to be clustered around the entrance instead of the reception desk, but every institution does things in its own way.

We make our way into the dining room, where some hotel guests – including the Frenchman who was plying Lianna with drink last night – are sitting at tables. No one seems to have had their breakfast served to them yet. Perhaps we are too early.

Aileen and Senga are sitting at a table for four, so we go to join them. On our way over, we chorus *Good Morning* to Valerie and Yvonne, who are sitting with the two hand-holding young men from the train – they are on our package tour as well.

Then I see the fat businessman sitting alone, smoking. Before breakfast! What a way to begin the day, smoking like a chimney! But out of politeness, I acknowledge him with a little wave.

Hardly have we begun to sit down, we haven't said a word to Aileen and Senga yet, when a gendarme bustles in, followed by Ferghal and the Major. This morning, the Major is not in uniform. He's wearing a smart suit.

Odder and odder. But I have no time to wonder, for the gendarme waves them to the nearest table and produces a pointer from somewhere; perhaps the hotel keeps a store of them for use by convention attendees. He raps against the wall for attention. "I am Inspector Clermont."

The Inspector's English is flawless and he doesn't waste words. Charlie Stout was killed last night. We are all suspects. The chief suspect, he moves the pointer to her, is Lianna.

The businessman asks calmly what happened. The Inspector tells us all that Mr Stout was strangled and his body thrown from the top of the Eiffel Tower. "Just as Miss Stuart wishes, no? He was strangled, he was throttled, every bone in his body was broken."

I am shocked by his callous disregard for Yvonne's feelings. But she looks as calm as always.

"This is complete nonsense." I say, in the same tone I'd use to freeze a girl who was giving me some ridiculous excuse for not having done her homework. "Miss Stuart cannot possibly be the culprit. She's afraid of heights. She couldn't have thrown Mr Stout from the top of the Eiffel Tower. Miss Stuart couldn't even have set foot on the top of the Eiffel Tower; she'd have collapsed before she could get that high."

"Yes, yeesss, perhaps. We will check."

The man seems to be quite reasonable. I begin to think that maybe the Prime Minister is right, and Britain should join the European Community after all. And Harold Wilson, who was our Prime Minister until just a few weeks ago, thought the same way.

I should have realised that when two men as clever as Edward Heath and Harold Wilson for once agree on something, then they'd be right.

"Meantime we will impound Miss Stuart's *passeport*, no?"

A sensible compromise. Lianna nods. I nod.

"Yeeess, but Miss Stuart's *passeport* is not in the hôtel safe. Miss Stuart has flouted our regulation, she did not give up her *passeport*. Why?"

Lianna looks bewildered. I realise why. She has never been near the reception desk. She doesn't know about having to give up her passport. I think back to the last time I saw Lianna's passport, when we boarded the ferry. She put it into the top of her smallest suitcase. Her little case was in the pile of luggage sitting beside me as I checked in, now piled up in our room.

As briefly as I can, I explain it all. The Inspector's lip curls, but he nods. He blows a whistle. Instantly, another gendarme comes through the door, to whom his pointer indicates our table. The gendarme moves towards us.

"So, Miss Stuart, you will give to my man your room key and the key to this travelling case, no?" Lianne nods eagerly and pulls a keyring out of her bag, selects the right key, and holds it up. But I know she doesn't have a room key. Before the Inspector can curl his lip at us again, I hand over my giant brass key fob. I point to the engraved numbers. "Room 101."

The gendarme takes the keys and leaves.

"Now, we move on. Miss Stuart, do you know anyone in Paris? Have you met or spoken to anyone at all since arriving in Paris, who is not in this room?"

He points again, and our waiter from last night moves forward. I look for the Maître d'. He is not in the room. Then I realise: he had gone off duty by the time we brought Lianna into the dining room with us to eat. The Inspector's pointer moves, and the hotel manager who was filling in for the barman last night steps forward. Again the pointer moves, points, and now we all look at the powder room attendant.

Lianna looks around slowly. She is confused, I can see. I think that she is shaking her head more in confusion than in agreement that everyone she has met is present, but indeed, who *could* she have met since arriving in Paris who is not in this room?

"We move on." He speaks briefly in rapid French. "Non." says the waiter. "Non." says the hotel manager. "Non." says the man who was buying Lianna drinks. "Non." says the powder room attendant.

"Now, Miss Stuart, I have asked these people if any of them were with you, saw you, or spoke to you, between 8:50 p.m. and 10:15 p.m. last night. They say No. Do you say Yes?"

Lianna shakes her head and whispers "No."

"We move on. I do not believe that anyone in this room was with you between 8:50 p.m. and 10:15 p.m. last night. If anyone wishes to challenge my belief, let him speak now."

I am not yet fearful for Lianna, because my mind is occupied by the annoying way Inspector Clermont chooses to express himself. He's so pompous. And doesn't he realise that "let **him** speak" is not what nice people say in these enlightened times when they are talking in mixed company?

"I challenge." I say it automatically.

And then I realise that I *can't* – because I don't know exactly when Lianna went off to the powder room, but it was probably before a quarter to nine. And I don't know exactly when we found Lianna in the bar, but it was near a quarter past ten...

"Yes?" Inspector Clermont is all polite interest.

I do my best. "That man" – I point at him – "was with Miss Stuart earlier than quarter past ten last night. He was drinking in the bar with her."

But Lianna is sadly shaking her head. And the Inspector's lip is curling again.

"Ah, but no, Miss Maguire. Monsieur joined Miss Stuart at exactly 10:16 p.m. You and Mrs Stout arrived at 10:17 p.m. He would certainly have liked to drink with Miss Stuart, but he was given no opportunity to do so."

I have wronged Lianna. She did not forget that she is a lady, at least not so far as to permit a stranger to buy her a drink.

And then the implication hits me. Last night Lianna disappeared for just under an hour and a half, and this man thinks that was time enough for her to have killed Charlie Stout.

The gendarme returns, and brings the keys not to us, but to the Inspector. They have a rapid low-voiced conversation in French.

"Miss Stuart, your *passeport* is not in any of your luggage. It is not anywhere visible in the room. Miss Maguire, naturally my man has not searched your luggage. He did not have your permission; also it is locked. Do you say that Miss Stuart's *passeport* is in your possession?"

I shake my head.

"Ah. We cannot permit a chief suspect who is a foreign national to remain at liberty in Paris when we do not hold that person's *passeport*. Indeed, it is against regulations even when no crime has been committed." He blows his whistle again.

And as the gendarmes lead Lianna away with her hands cuffed behind her back, I recognise with some bitterness and some regret that my country's stance on the European Community is absolutely sound. We should keep these Frenchies as far away as we possibly can.

I only realise that I've said this out loud when the Major swivels toward me and barks out, "Quite right m'dear! Very well put! We should toddle down to the police station now and rescue your friend from those clots, should we not?"

Obviously I've got to go and see what I can do for poor Lianna, but I don't want company and particularly not his. It was this lunatic's rage which drove Lianna into the frenzy that has brought her under suspicion.

However, the Major continues, "It's very unusual for a gendarme to speak English as well as that Inspector does. How's your French, dear lady? I don't normally mention it, no sense in letting the side down, but I speak French like a native. I was stationed here during the war, y'know."

I was starting primary school when World War 2 was ending. However, his French is better than mine, and he certainly owes Lianna any help he can give her.

We toddle down to the police station.

In what feels like no time, we're sitting in an interview room with an Inspector Toussaint, whose English is very good. But I'm not under any illusion that by myself I could have achieved the same result. Major Peverel is very efficient. And for some reason, the Major is respected here.

Inspector Toussaint explains the French system to me. They have something called a *dossier*.

French officials get a *dossier* together by asking anyone they like a lot of questions. Everyone must answer, but the official is not allowed to criticise or query the answers.

They can only ask another person if that person agrees or disagrees with the answers given; and what their own answers are.

This explains why Inspector Clermont spoke in that odd, pompous way.

He asked his questions, he got answers, he gave Lianna and me an opportunity to contradict what he had heard. I suppose that given the peculiar French system, he's been quite fair.

In the old days, Inspector Toussaint tells me, the *dossier* would take days and days to get, with everyone sitting in court in front of a magistrate and writing down all the questions and answers in longhand. Now a suitable official takes the *dossier*.

The purpose of a *dossier* is to get all the facts clear. If new facts come to light, there will be another hearing, and everything about the new facts will be recorded too.

Sometimes the official is an Inspector in the gendarmes. Or maybe some outside expert takes the *dossier*. Or an official in another department.

If the *dossier* shows that the suspect could not have committed the crime, then the suspect goes free. The case is closed against that person and it is not re-opened.

But if a *dossier* shows that most certainly the suspect could have committed the crime, then the suspect is brought to trial.

If the facts show that it's quite likely that the suspect could have committed the crime, then just as we do, the French will consider whether there is a big flight risk danger. If they think that there is a big risk, then the suspect gets locked up until he or she is brought before a magistrate who decides whether that person can be free until trial or will stay locked up.

Inspector Toussaint is being kind to me, but he makes it quite clear that unless Lianna's passport is surrendered, she will stay locked up. And because the passport wasn't where it should have been, maybe she will stay locked up anyway. Lianna's passport is missing; the French police do not like that. The longer it stays missing, the less likely they will be to believe that it went missing in an innocent way.

The only ray of hope, so far as I can see, is new facts coming to light. And so I ask the Inspector when he thinks the next *dossier* hearing will be. He coughs and gets embarrassed.

There is only a second *dossier* hearing, he explains, when something very unusual happens, something which makes it obvious that significant facts were missed first time around.

By various polite circumlocutions, he gets me to understand that the Sûreté Nationale do not believe that significant facts have been missed, and are not out there looking for new facts.

I ask if I will be allowed to bring Lianna clothes and books and any other comforts.

Inspector Toussaint gives me a list of forbidden items. He says that I can visit every day, and bring Lianna anything that's not on the forbidden list. He also says that I can ask for him at the police station entrance desk anytime because he will help me if he can.

I ask for a copy of the *dossier* and he gets one run off for me. When they bring me my copy, they also bring one for the Major. He is respected here; I suddenly feel sure that without his help, I would have not have been given my own copy of the *dossier*.

Inspector Toussaint's last words, intended to comfort me, come as a huge shock.

"Do not worry, your friend will be quite safe. She will put in the defence of *Crime Passionnel*. She is a woman of great passion, many witnesses will attest to this. She goes on impulse to see the Eiffel Tower, which many have heard her admire. There, unexpectedly, she finds the man she hates, who has given her excellent cause to hate him. In a moment of overmastering passion, she kills him. She will be acquitted on this defence. In a year or so, she will be able to put all this behind her and return to Scotland."

As we leave the police station, the Major offers me a cup of tea. I laugh bitterly. *French so-called tea on top of everything else,* I think. *No thanks!*

"No, no, dear lady," remonstrates the Major. "I promise you some real tea. I've put up at the out-of-the-way little place where I'm staying because I can get proper English tea there." He notices my frown and adds hastily, "British tea, I mean."

The Major's idea of an out-of-the-way little place turns out to be the most palatial hotel that I have ever seen. We go through to a beautiful public room full of comfortable sofas. But it doesn't have a bar and it doesn't have restaurant fittings either. In fact, I've never seen anything like it.

A waiter in a tail-coat glides in and places a little set of tables in front of the three sofas in a semi-circle where the Major has paused. We sit. A second waiter appears almost instantly, carrying a tray on which there is a teapot, teacups and saucers, spoons, sugar and milk, lemon slices, an empty hot water jug, slops bowl, a very small tea-caddy, and an electric kettle!

As if it were the most ordinary thing in the world, the first waiter takes the kettle, finds a wall socket, and plugs it in, whilst the second lays out the tea things. He takes the slops bowl, a spoon, the teapot, and tea-caddy over to the first waiter, who warms the pot and then plugs in the kettle again. When the water is bubbly boiling, tea is ceremoniously made, and the teapot placed in front of the Major.

By this time, a third waiter has arrived with little side plates, cake knives and forks, and a 2-tier cake stand crammed with cakes. These are placed beside the teapot just as the second waiter comes over with linen napkins, which he opens onto our laps with a flourish.

All three waiters stand near the Major, beaming at him. "We might as well be comfortable." he says "D'ye fancy a sandwich?" I shake my head and he flicks a hand at the waiters, who glide out as silently as they glided in. "Will you be mother, m'dear?" I pour the tea.

It is the best tea I have ever tasted, a glorious golden Ceylon. Even in my anguish for Lianna, I take comfort from the taste and feel of that tea. We drink silently.

"Now, I'll help you if I can, Miss Maguire. What's your plan?"

Even after a reviving cup of tea, I'm still too upset to understand things quickly.

What plan is he talking about? But all I say is, "Do please call me Màiri."

"And I'm Ellis. Now that we're friends, how can I help you, Màiri?"

Sometimes the classless society isn't all it's cracked up to be. I suppose it's natural enough that a man as old school as the Major would take an invitation to call me by my first name as the beginning of a friendship; he's probably never even heard of the classless society.

"Major," I begin hesitantly

"Ellis."

Well, I asked for that one.

"Ellis, I don't know what you mean. It's Lianna who needs help."

"Of course. I meant, how can I be of most use to you in your plan to get her freed?"

"Plan? I don't have any plan..."

"Ah yes, you haven't read the *dossier* yet. You want to study it before forming your plan."

"Ellis, I'm a school teacher, not a master criminal. I can't break Lianna out of jail!"

"Wouldn't do any good if you did, they'd catch her at the border. Best border team I know. No, you'll have to prove her innocence, of course. How can I help? Yours to command, dear lady, I assure you."

Best border team he knows? And why does the Sûreté respect him? Who is this man? "The Sûreté wouldn't have given me that *dossier* if you hadn't asked them to, would they, Ellis?"

"Certainly, they would! Always play a straight bat, those fellows! Of course they would have given you the case papers!" And then he adds with a secret little grin, "In a few days or so..."

He reaches across and pats my shoulder awkwardly. "Buck up, Màiri. I have to follow your lead, my dear girl. I don't know your friend at all, so it's up to you to think this one through. But if she killed that scoundrel of a taxman, I'm no judge of character" – he winks – "and they don't call me 'Gimlet' for nothing!"

"You don't understand, Ellis" I wail. "She did vanish for well over an hour last night. Her passport has vanished too! Of course I know that she didn't kill Charlie Stout, but how could I ever convince anyone else of that? I'm just a school teacher, not a detective! And I have to get on a train to Istanbul in under seven days time!"

I break down, sobbing and wiping angrily at my eyes.

The Major sits back. "Then you'll have to crack this case in the next six days, won't you?"

The More I Learn, The Less I Know

Chapter 5 The More I Learn, The Less I Know

11:00 a.m. Saturday, 15th August 1970

Hôtel Marquis, Rue Greneta, Paris, France

The Major is a dangerous lunatic, but he's right.

How can I call myself Lianna's best friend and then just sit here crying when she needs me to be strong for her? I get out my hankie and wipe my eyes, and then I pour us both another cup of tea. Perhaps it will help me to think.

I begin thinking out loud. "Someone killed Charlie Stout. Unless there's a serial killer on the loose, the killer wanted to put Stout out of action. Now that might be because he got into a dispute with some local hard man, but let's face it, he didn't have much time to get into a new fight, he'd only been here a couple of hours when he was killed."

The Major has the *dossier* open and I appeal to him for corroboration. "Is that right?"

He nods. "Within the time frame, yes. By medical guestimate, he was killed within one and a half to three hours of his arrival; and by reference to his known movements probably closer to an hour and a half."

I need to find out where Lianna had actually been during the time frame. She couldn't really have vanished and therefore she must have been somewhere.

I go on thinking aloud...

"So it's unlikely that this was a new quarrel. The killer probably followed him here. But there are a lot of places the killer could have followed him *from* and our Charlie is not a man who was well-liked. The killer might even have been living here in Paris and just happened to see Charlie in the street. Or if the killer followed him, then the following could have been done in a lot of different *ways*."

The Major frowns. "I don't see that, m'dear. Might have spotted him in the street, yes. Bit of a coincidence, but it could happen. Known it to happen, in fact, with another man. But never mind that. The point is, if he was followed, he could only have been followed on the train."

"True, but he could have been followed on the train in a lot of different ways."

I begin ticking off some ways on my fingers:

Index finger.. "The killer might have known that he was coming on this tour, and come ahead of him, and been waiting for him in the tour hotel or at Gare du Nord."

I interrupt my finger-ticking for a moment to drink more tea. It really is scrumptious tea. After a moment of savouring my tea, I put down the cup and begin finger-ticking again.

Middle finger. "Or the killer might have had a partner on the train, a traveller or a railway employee, who sent a telegram – or something – saying that Stout was on the train."

Ring finger. "Or the killer might have been a traveller or a railway employee on the train...

Pinkie. "... or it could be that the killer spotted Stout on the train by coincidence and followed him after that. So the killer could have been on the train, or at the station, or at the hotel, or chance-met in the street, or even chance-met at the Eiffel Tower. That's a lot of possible killers!"

My head is exploding so I stop for another sip of tea.

The Major has pulled out a little leather notebook. He turns his notebook around so that I can see it. He has drawn columns across the pages. They are headed:

TRAIN	STATION	STREET	HOTEL	TOWER
Williams	Brown	Reilly	Mrs S	Valerie
Orville			Aileen	

"These people were on the train. Tour Guide was the last to see Stout alive. At the Tower. Others saw Stout at the station, in the street, at the hotel. So they say. All in the *dossier*."

"What about Senga? She was on the train."

"Short-sighted. Broke her spectacles. Couldn't recognise her friend without 'em, never mind Stout. So she says. Friend agrees."

I sip some more tea.

"Well, we have to start somewhere. Let's talk to these people. And I'd like to draw up a list of who was where when, because when I have to wade through all these different statements in the *dossier*, then I think it gets a bit confusing.

"And after that, Ellis, if I may, I'm going to take Lianna some of your wonderful tea."

The Major summons the gliding waiters again.

While they are making fresh tea, the Major makes me a gift of a small leather-covered notebook, a bit like his, except the cover on mine is a pale tan, almost like the dull yellow thread in the Maguire plaid. People talk a lot about a Maguire tartan, but traditionally there is only the plaid. It's the Scots who have tartans as well as plaids. Lianna's clan has *three*.

The Major and I do a lot of scribbling down of places and times on-to some sheets of hotel notepaper, and then I carefully copy the results we have worked out into my new notebook.

Murder Time-frame based on times recorded in the *dossier*

Time of Death	9:30 p.m. to 11:30 p.m.		on medical evidence
	8:16 p.m.	8:30 p.m.	8:45 p.m.
Major Peverel	gets taxi	British Embassy	
Harry Brown	walking home	arrives home	home all night
Ferghal Reilly	walking home	8:25 p.m. home	eats at home
Aileen & Senga	walking to hotel	hotel check in	check in ends
Jimmy Orville	walking to hotel	hotel queue	checks in
Rhys Williams	walking to hotel	hotel queue	hotel queue
Màiri	walking to hotel	hotel queue	hotel queue
Lianna	walking to hotel	hotel queue	hotel queue
Charlie Stout	walking to hotel	hotel queue	Tower
Yvonne Stout	walking to hotel	hotel queue	hotel queue
Valerie	walking to hotel	leaves tour	Tower

	9:00 p.m.	9:15 p.m.	9:30 p.m.	9:43 p.m.
Major Peverel	British Embassy	leaves at 11 p.m.		
Harry Brown	his wife alibis			
Ferghal Reilly	arrives casino	leaves at midnight		
Aileen & Senga	in their room	rest of night		
Jimmy Orville	check in ends	in his room	rest of night	
Rhys Williams	checks in	check in ends	visits JO	in bed
Màiri	hotel queue	checks in	Dining	
Lianna	leaves 8:50 p.m.	*her whereabouts unknown until 10:15 p.m.*		
Charlie Stout	Eiffel Tower		He Dies	
Yvonne Stout	hotel queue	hotel queue	checks in	Dining
Valerie	at Eiffel Tower	leaves 9:10 p.m.		

I also copy over into a fresh page in my lovely notebook the columns that the Major had written out of where people had seen Mr Stout.

Working all that out takes a while to do, and by the time I've finished, the waiters have made a fresh pot of tea and decanted it into a vacuum flask.

But I'm not ready to leave just yet. I'm too nosy not to ask how come the Major was at the British Embassy all of last night?

"Oh, just a spot of dinner, m'dear. School chum of mine is the naval attaché there; always try to catch up with him when I'm in Paris. Bit of a knees up last night. That's why I was in dress uniform. I'm in the Reserves, y'know."

I'm not fooled. If twenty-five bright eager teenagers all backing each other up can't pull the wool over my eyes, it's not likely that one frail old man can. The Major is Up To Something.

But I must go and see Lianna, so whatever he's hiding will just have to stay hidden for now. I'll get the story out of him later.

We agree to meet up again at four o'clock, at the Hôtel Albert. The Major says we can try to find some of the people on our lists then, and ask them to talk to us. Somehow, I feel sure that there won't be any "try" about it. The Major will see to it, in some hidden way, that anyone he wants to talk to just happens to be there when he arrives. But why does he care about freeing my friend?

I pick up the flask of tea and some of the little cakes too, and go to see Lianna.

But the gendarmes won't let me see Lianna with the tea flask, or let her have the cakes.

I ask for Inspector Toussaint.

They put me in a waiting room. The Inspector comes there quite soon. He explains that the wee flask of tea is forbidden because forbidden substances could be dissolved in the tea, and there is a similar objection to the cakes.

"Me and Lianna aren't into the psychedelic scene, Inspector, honestly. But in Paris you can't get the kind of tea British people drink, and so Major Peverel has it specially made for him. He kindly sent his tea to Lianna to cheer her up. Tea isn't on the forbidden list you gave me. And Inspector, you said she might be here *for a year*. You surely won't deny her a mouthful of tea in all that time. I thought that it might put some heart into her..."

I've pulled out all the stops. Now we'll see just how much weight Major Peverel carries around here. The Inspector takes the flask from me. He shakes his head.

"Ah, Miss Maguire, you beautiful British ladies, you must learn to live without your tea. Take coffee, it is a much better drink." He sends for coffee, and then for Lianna.

A tray arrives with a full coffee pot, cups and saucers, milk and sugar. Then Lianna is brought in.

The Inspector pours out coffee for me and for himself, but into Lianna's cup he pours tea out of the flask. He really is a very kind man.

Inspector Toussaint explains to Lianna about the *dossier,* and Lianna, having a good business head on her, understands at once.

Then he says we may have thirty minutes to talk alone, and after that Lianna can make a list for me of things she wants me to bring her. He will look over the list and tell me what I'm allowed to bring.

It all sounds pretty good to me. I realise how lucky we are that the Major has been able to persuade Inspector Toussaint to interest himself in Lianna's case. He leaves us alone.

Tristan Toussaint comes into his office just as the phone starts ringing. "Oui?"

An English voice on the other end "They've just left London. Have you men at the airport?"

"But of a certainty, my dear confrère, I always have men at the airport."

"Never mind that! I meant, do you have some men at Orly on the lookout for this lot?"

"Of course. How could it be otherwise, when it is Scotland Yard who asks this favour of us?"

I can give Lianna a big hug at last. And we cry into each other's shoulders for a little while.

But I mustn't waste this time when we can talk, and so after a bit I push her back into her seat.

"Lianna, we have to get you out of here. The poliss are convinced that you killed Charlie Stout. Where were you for all that time last night? What were you really doing?"

She's embarrassed. "I fell asleep. I was tired and you told me to go sit down and I did, and then I fell asleep."

I can see that she's leaving something out. I need to know what.

"Yes, but where? You weren't in the lobby, you weren't in the room. Anyway, you didn't have the room key."

Oh, she's embarrassed all right. She thinks I'm going to say that she shouldn't have done whatever it was she did. But the stakes are too high for me to start moralising, doesn't she know that? Maybe not, her face is turned away from me.

I stroke her arm. "Lianna, love, you were tired, you wanted to sit down, isn't that right?" She nods. "And you couldn't find a seat in the lobby, and anyway it was noisy." She nods. "And you didn't go into the bar, not at first, because you had only been there a minute when we found you. So where did you go first, love?"

It was like pulling teeth, but I got out of her where she had been.

The Famous
French Food

Chapter 6 The Famous French Food

12:15 p.m. Saturday, 15th August, 1970

Lucky 8 Casino, Rue du Faubourg Saint-Denis, Paris, France

Harry Brown does not approve of the French habit of drinking wine all the time, especially not at meals, where it interferes with the great taste of good solid North of England cooking. Amélie, his wife, does not agree.

So around noon on Saturday, whilst Màiri is struggling with the French legal system, Harry is tucking into Lancashire hotpot all by himself. His meal is interrupted by the unwelcome news that a British lady has asked to see him.

Harry doesn't know many Brits who are in Paris just now, and a visit from any one of them means trouble. Well, the trouble is not going to spoil his lunch.

A true leader controls time. He does not permit unexpected events to control him.

"Give her some chips and ask her to play the tables for half an hour. I'll see her in a bit. If she won't wait, ask her to come back another day."

Twenty minutes later, his hotpot scarfed down, Harry lights a Benson & Hedges and strolls into the casino, where he discovers Aileen McPherson drooping over the roulette wheel. An unexpected and irritating complication. She'll have come about Stout. Again.

I'm walking back to the hotel when I spot Valerie sitting by herself at a pavement café. I'm meeting the Major at four o'clock, but that's hours away. A late lunch with Valerie is just what my tummy needs. Maybe she can help me to get to the bottom of all the craziness.

I say *Hello* to Valerie and begin to sit, and a waiter is instantly there, pulling out the seat for me with one hand and handing me a huge *carte* with the other. I wave it away. "*Café au lait et un Croque Monsieur, s'il vous plait.*"

I'm proud that I can order my own lunch, not needing Valerie to order for me, even if it is just a ham and cheese sandwich. Then I'm ashamed of preening myself on schoolgirl French when poor Lianna's life is hanging in the balance.

The French still have Capital Punishment, you see, and Lianna won't enter a defence of *Crime Passionnel*. I ken fine she won't, because she didn't kill Charlie Stout – and Lianna is very prim and proper when she's not in the grip of her temper. She won't admit to a crime she didn't commit, not her.

I think that the best thing I can do is fill Valerie in on what has happened so far today, so I do. She goes paper-white with shock and sympathy for Lianna.

I'm thinking what a nice person Valerie is when the waiter appears again, putting onto the table in rapid succession some cutlery wrapped in a paper napkin, a cup of coffee, a little sugar bowl, and a tiny paper serviette on top of which he places a glass of iced water.

How can he *do* all that so fast without a tray to carry the things on?

"Valerie, I was wondering, can you help me with this?"

I show her the page where I've copied the Major's list into my new notebook.

TRAIN	STATION	STREET	HOTEL	TOWER
Williams	Brown	Reilly	Mrs S	Valerie
Orville			Aileen	

"The *dossier* says you were the last person to see Charlie Stout alive, when he was going to the Eiffel Tower. These people were on the train, the *dossier* says, and they saw Mr Stout at the station, in the street, or at the hotel. Would you talk to me a wee bit about that?"

"Yes, I will help all I can. Mr Stout did want to go to the Eiffel Tower. That is true. I did not know the Sûreté have put in the *dossier* that I am the last one to have seen him alive."

The waiter arrives with my Croque Monsieur, so I tuck my notebook back into my handbag.

"Yes, there is a lot that the Sûreté don't talk about much, Valerie, even if it is in the *dossier*. So I hope that whatever you can tell me will help poor Lianna. I hope we can get a second *dossier* hearing if we can bring new facts to light."

"Màiri, there is not often a second *dossier* hearing, but I will help you all I can." Tears are standing in her eyes at the thought of what Lianna is going through. Valerie is such a kind person! I can see that she really feels for poor Lianna, whom she hardly knows.

"Who could have imagined that so much trouble would come from his death? It is too bad that he came here!" A spasm of anger? irritation? regret? crosses her sweet face.

The odd expression is gone too quickly for me to be sure what Valerie was feeling just then, but something about the way she had looked is a little unsettling...

...and how strangely she said: "...too bad that he came here" almost as if she were complaining of Charlie Stout's arrival in Paris rather than politely regretting his death.

"So yes, I went to the Eiffel Tower last night, because Mr Stout asked me to tell him the way there, and also I needed to collect the tickets for our group to visit the Tower this evening, so I am going to the Tower in my car even without him."

"We're going to visit the Eiffel Tower as a group tonight?" I hadn't known that. It may be useful. The killer may show some sign of guilt.

"Yes, the group always does."

I interrupt Valerie before she can continue, because I'm thinking about the people whose movements the Major had noted down from the *dossier* files. I don't know all of them.

Maybe Valerie knows them; she seems to know a lot of people.

"Valerie, who are Williams, Orville, and Brown? Do you know?"

She frowns. "Brown, no. Rhys Williams is on our tour, he was in the dining carriage with us on the train. A Welshman. He sat with his friend, Jimmy Orville. Jimmy is a ladies' clothes wholesaler. They live in London."

Progress! I remember now that when I saw them on the train, there was something about the Welshman's friend which had brought Carnaby Street to the front of my mind.

For the first time, I begin to let myself hope that I may be able to notice enough things to find out some new facts, and get Lianna a second hearing!

What a good thing that the Major had thought of making that note.

"Thanks, Valerie. And we know Ferghal, of course. Do you have a phone number for him? Could we ring him up and ask him to come down to the hotel to see us?"

I already have a telephone number for Ferghal (I got it from Lianna) but I want to see how friendly Valerie is with him.

She laughs. "Is there any ex-pat in Paris who doesn't have Ferghal's number? He is such a sociable man."

Ex-pat is an abbreviation for expatriate. That's the word the English use to describe anyone who lives and works in a country which isn't the same country where that person is a citizen.

The English are so much in the habit of taking over the world that it never occurs to them that anyone would use any word for anything except their word. And because it never occurs to them, it hardly ever occurs to anyone else.

I suddenly realise that I am an ex-pat now. I've left Scotland and soon I will be living and working in Turkey. And so will Lianna, even if the French do have her locked up right now.

I wonder why it is that Valerie thinks of herself as an ex-pat. She might not, of course. She may just be explaining how easy it is to get Ferghal's number.

But there's a bell ringing at the back of my mind, I have a notion that this may be important. I almost dig out my notebook from my handbag again, but I need both hands for eating my Croque Monsieur and I don't want it to get cold. It's so delicious!

I'll come back to whether Valerie is a Brit or not later...

Màiri's Mental Note: Is Valerie a British Ex-Pat?

"So maybe Ferghal will take a drink with us? Or come with our group to the Tower?"

"Both, I should think. I'll ask him."

"Valerie, it says in the *dossier* that you went with Charlie Stout to the Tower at half-past eight last night? And that you didn't see him again after you got there?"

"That's right. I went straight to the booth to collect our group's tickets, and then I came away. I went home and had a bite of supper."

But that can't be right.

The train got in at 8:16 p.m.

We got to the Hôtel Albert around half-past eight, and then the check-in queue formed.

Yvonne had said that her husband was with her at the hotel just before she'd joined the queue. She was behind me in the queue, and I had been in the queue at least twenty minutes when she joined it, maybe longer.

That means that Charlie Stout didn't leave Hôtel Albert for the Tower until around a quarter to nine, and if the times in the *dossier* are right, probably he left the Hôtel Albert about ten to nine. I'm surprised enough to put down my knife and fork and scrabble through my bag.

When I find my notebook and dig it out of my bag again, I flip rapidly through the pages to check. Yes, there the times are, set out just as I thought.

Murder Time-frame based on times recorded in the *dossier*

Time of Death	9:30 p.m. to 11:30 p.m.		on medical evidence

	8:16 p.m.	8:30 p.m.	8:45 p.m.
Major Peverel	gets taxi	British Embassy	
Harry Brown	walking home	arrives home	home all night
Ferghal Reilly	walking home	8:25 p.m. home	eats at home
Aileen & Senga	walking to hotel	hotel check in	check in ends
Jimmy Orville	walking to hotel	hotel queue	checks in
Rhys Williams	walking to hotel	hotel queue	hotel queue
Màiri	walking to hotel	hotel queue	hotel queue
Lianna	walking to hotel	hotel queue	hotel queue
Charlie Stout	walking to hotel	hotel queue	Tower
Yvonne Stout	walking to hotel	hotel queue	hotel queue
Valerie	walking to hotel	leaves tour	Tower

	9:00 p.m.	9:15 p.m.	9:30 p.m.	9:43 p.m.
Major Peverel	British Embassy	leaves at 11 p.m.		
Harry Brown	his wife alibis			
Ferghal Reilly	arrives casino	leaves at midnight		
Aileen & Senga	in their room	rest of night		
Jimmy Orville	check in ends	in his room	rest of night	
Rhys Williams	checks in	check in ends	visits JO	in bed
Màiri	hotel queue	checks in	Dining	
Lianna	leaves 8:50 p.m.	her whereabouts unknown until 10:15 p.m.		
Charlie Stout	Eiffel Tower		He Dies	
Yvonne Stout	hotel queue	hotel queue	checks in	Dining
Valerie	at Eiffel Tower	leaves 9:10 p.m.		

Well, it's only a few minutes difference, nothing to fuss about. And my food is getting cold! Quickly laying my notebook on the table, I savour another mouthful. Yummy!

"OK. So the *dossier* says you last saw him alive around nine o'clock?" But that *can't* be right. It must have been quarter past nine or later. Yet Valerie is nodding.

How odd... well, she had a lot to do, she was rushing around, probably she wasn't looking at her watch.

The last crumb of my Croque Monsieur is gone. It was the best ham and cheese sandwich I've ever tasted. But it's nearly three o'clock now and I want to get to the bank to cash some Travellers Cheques before I meet the Major at four, and I still have to pay for my lunch.

I need to hurry.

So I just make a quick note in the little notebook to remind myself to check the times more carefully later and pop the notebook back into my bag.

Màiri's Note: Check the time Tax Charlie left our hotel

Then I thank Valerie for her company and rush off. She looks rather sad.

H arry Brown isn't happy. He puffs disconsolately on his fag, and lights another from its tip. Chain smoking. Amélie would give him what-for if she were here.

She never is here. Harry does not approve of a wife's presence in her husband's office; and besides, he needs a respite from her nagging.

He worries that it was a mistake to give Ferghal his current assignment, despite his popularity with the weaker sex.

Ferghal got Magatte away safely, granted. That Scotswoman was eating out of his hand, true.

Not Ferghal's fault that the gendarmes arrested her, but he should have finished the job long before that happened. He's flighty, lazy, unreliable.

And now Aileen has turned up again, weeping about that blackmailing little sod of a taxman and expecting him to sort it out. As if he doesn't have troubles enough of his own right now, without Aileen asking him to take care of her, just as if it hadn't been six years or more since he last saw her!

She had been good to him when he was in the nick though, came every Visiting Day, always remembered to bring him a carton of Benson & Hedges. She never brought him the cheaper brands, even when money was tight for her. So he will take care of her troubles, but later. Now is not the time for complications.

Why couldn't Magatte have given Ferghal a clearer signal?

Harry distrusts Ferghal's ability to gain access discreetly to Room 101. He does not feel good about the chances of Ferghal managing to lay his hands on the package Magatte hid in one of that teacher's suitcases. He feels, in short, that the job is too hard for Ferghal.

But how hard can it be, for a charmer like Ferghal, to gain the trust of a dozy little teacher?

I keep my eyes peeled for a bank on my way back to the Hôtel Albert, and I soon see a big corner building with the words **Banque Populaire** in absolutely gigantic letters on its glass windows. The words **Banque Populaire** are repeated in huge brass letters on the sign above its storefront. "Banque" is the French word for a bank.

When I get inside, I'm relieved to see that the queue is short. They have a little counter to one side where you can write out deposit slips – or in my case sign Travellers Cheques so that I can cash them – before you join the queue waiting to be served.

So I turn towards the side counter and there's Senga. She's holding her book of Traveller's Cheques up to her eyes and peering at them. It's obvious that she wants to get some French money; but she can't see her cheques well enough to be able to sign them properly.

I see in a flash that what the Major read in the *dossier* is absolutely correct. Senga is very short-sighted. She's broken her specs, and without them, she can't see a yard in front of her.

If she broke her specs before the time that Charlie Stout was killed, then she couldn't have been the one who killed him.

But after all, we don't know when she broke her specs, do we? She might have killed him, and this might be her cunning alibi. Although if

I'd been the killer, I'd have made certain that I had a better alibi – not being able to see is so very inconvenient.

"Hello, Senga."

"Oh, hello, Màiri! I'm sorry, I didn't see you there, I'm blind as a bat without my glasses. Thank Heavens Aileen has found an optician who can make me a new pair. But they aren't ready yet, of course. So I'm struggling a bit with these cheques."

I see loose cheques lying on the floor and pick them up for her. Senga doesn't even notice; she can't see clearly enough to know what it is that I'm holding. I look at the denominations. Ouch! More than a month's salary, and Senga doesn't even know that she's dropped them.

"Senga." I hold out her Travellers Cheques to her. "How much money do you want to cash?"

"A few hundred francs I think."

I put a couple of cheques on the counter. "Then sign these ones I've put on the counter for you. But put the rest of them in your bag first."

Senga puts the Travellers Cheques she was peering at into her handbag, still not realising that I'm standing there with a fistful of her money.

"These too." I push the Travellers Cheques I'm holding into her hand. "You dropped them."

"Oh, Màiri, did I? What a lucky thing for me that you're here."

I shake my head. "How long have you been as short-sighted as this, Senga?"

"Oh, since I was little. I can't see at all without my glasses. To me, you're a sort of people-shaped blur. I know that you're you because I recognise your voice, but I can't actually see you properly."

We've moved into the queue and in a minute we'll be at the teller's window.

"How did you come to break them?"

She's just a little cross now, understandably so considering how hard it is for her to manage without her specs.

"We were going up to the room. The bellboy sort of banged into Aileen, and she sort of fell into me, and I happened to be cleaning my glasses at the time. I dropped them, and they fell down a few steps and hit an urn in the stairwell and smashed up. It was pretty grim. But not really anybody's fault, of course."

She's reached the teller and is drawing her francs. The next window opens and I go there to draw mine. But I don't have my passport for them to check my signature against, so they won't give me any francs.

I notice that Senga does have her passport. She gets her francs and puts her money into her bag carefully this time and we start walking together towards the doors to the outside.

The loss of her specs is weighing on her mind, and she's still talking about it.

"They were my spare pair of glasses. Only a couple of minutes earlier, that man who was murdered had knocked my normal ones out of my hand and trodden on them, bending them all out of shape. So I got my spares out of my suitcase and I was just cleaning them, I hadn't even put them on yet, when they got broken too. Really, I feel as if this trip has been jinxed!"

I'm pole-axed. Charlie Stout had broken her specs just before she and Aileen had completed their check-in! Then he couldn't have been at the Eiffel Tower at nine o'clock. I must add that to the time frame grid.

Màiri's Mental Note: Tax Charlie was at the front of our hotel queue at 8:45 p.m.

"You have been unlucky, haven't you?" I sympathise. "I thought you and Aileen were lucky to be the first ones checked in, but it turned out horrid for you with your specs getting broken like that. How did Mr Stout happen to knock them out of your hand?"

"Oh, he wasn't looking where he was going. He was talking to his wife, who was off to our left, and he was looking at her, not us, but he was walking in our direction at the same time, and he just breenged right into me, knocked the breath right out me, his whole body hit me so hard that my glasses fell right off my face, and then he stepped on them, and he didn't even say he was sorry, he didn't even look at what he'd done, he just walked right on past me as if nothing had happened." She's crying at the memory.

"Oh, Senga, I'm so sorry."

"I mustn't speak ill of the dead," Senga says, and I can see she would have said plenty if he'd still been alive. "But I just feel as if this whole trip has been jinxed! First I break my shoe heel getting down from the Inverness train, and then I nearly choke on an olive stone at Le Havre, and then there's that horrid incident on the Paris train, and all my glasses got broken last night. And if you hadn't walked into the bank when you did, I'd have lost my spending money too."

"Well, I hope I've broken the chain of bad luck for you!" I mean, what else could I say?

But my heart is singing, because I have **Two New Facts**.

Inspector Clermont's precious *dossier* is just plain wrong. The times are way off!

I can't wait to sit down with my copy of the *dossier* and work out just what happened "within the time frame" as the Major would put it, and then to march in on the poliss and tell them we need a new *dossier* hearing!

Because the times the current *dossier* records for Charlie Stout's movements are wrong.

And Lianna's whereabouts are not unknown, not anymore. I just want to find someone who saw her so as to be sure to satisfy Inspector Clermont that she was where she says she was.

But I need to get some more francs. I ask Senga how she got her passport back?

"Oh, the hotel gives it back to you after the police have inspected it. You need your passport for so many things here." She sighs, and I can see that she's regretting ever having left the Highlands. Then Senga says she's meeting Aileen in a café nearby. They're going shopping.

And I have to get back to the Hôtel Albert to meet the Major. But I'm a bit worried at the thought of Senga wandering around Paris on her own, and her not able to see anything.

"Are you sure you'll be all right? Where exactly are you meeting Aileen?" I'm thinking I'd better take her there, even if it does make me late. But at that very moment, Aileen bustles up.

"There you are, Senga! Why you couldn't have waited five minutes until I was done changing my clothes, instead of rushing off to the bank on your own, I do not know!"

But I can see that she isn't really worried, and she should be. Senga is her friend and she's all shaken up and not able to see well, so Aileen shouldn't be letting her wander around a strange city on her own.

I think to myself that she's not a very kind person. I mean, look how concerned Valerie was about poor Lianna, who is, after all, near to being a stranger to her. But Senga looks sheepish.

"I needed some air, Aileen." She's quite apologetic as she says it. "And I've been all right. Màiri came into the bank and she's been helping me."

I turn to Aileen. "Senga's been telling me that you found an optician who can make some new specs for her. Terrible bad luck that both pairs of her specs got broken last night."

"Yes, we were just about to go up to our room. The bellboy was picking up our luggage when that horrible taxman breenged right into her, nearly knocked her flying, and he did send her glasses flying. And then he stepped on them, the clumsy ox. Unless he did it on purpose, and I wouldn't put that past him. He's such a nasty piece of work, just a wee jumped-up keelie!"

Senga is shaking her head. "Aileen, Aileen, De mortuis nihil nisi bonum. Speak no ill of the dead."

So I say, "Well, it can be hard, Senga, if you've a ruinous tax bill. Poor Lianna got a terrible tax bill from him, and look where she is now. Was he your tax inspector too, Aileen?"

"No, no, I just heard Lianna carrying on, same as everyone else. Personally, I don't believe she killed him. If you're going to kill someone, you'd keep quiet about it, stands to reason."

But I'm thinking to be so bitter Aileen must have a reason of her own to hate Charlie Stout, and maybe it's a strong enough reason to kill for.

Mind, I don't know how she could have done it, because she was in her hotel room with Senga during the whole of the time period that Stout might have been killed. Possibly she had an accomplice.

I fish out my notebook and make a quick note to look into it.

Màiri's Note: Check Aileen's dossier notes. And find out her connection to Tax Charlie

Then I flip back a couple of pages to show them the page with Major's note of where Charlie Stout was last seen by whom.

TRAIN	STATION	STREET	HOTEL	TOWER
Williams	Brown	Reilly	Mrs S	Valerie
Orville			Aileen	

"Do you know Mr Brown?"

Aileen is shaking her head, but of course Senga can't see well enough to know that, and she innocently lands Aileen right in it. "I don't, but he was that businessman on the train, wasn't he? Aileen knows him quite well, don't you, Aileen?"

"I simply passed a few words with him on the train, out of common civility. I wouldn't say that I *know* him." Aileen's tone is cool, but she can't lie her way out of this one, not with Senga standing there with her mouth open.

I jot down a quick note.

Màiri's Note: Why is Aileen lying about Mr Brown? Did they conspire to kill Tax Charlie?

"Well, ladies, I must run. I'm supposed to be meeting Ferghal and I'm late."

I wave *Bye Bye* and hurry off to our hotel.

Màiri
Investigates

Chapter 7 Màiri Investigates

3:54 p.m. Saturday, 15th August, 1970

Hôtel Albert, Rue du Faubourg Saint-Denis, Paris, France

I didn't want Aileen to realise that the Major and me are working to-gether, so I made that up about meeting Ferghal, but it's a judge-ment on me not to lie, for I'm barely inside the Hôtel Albert lobby when Ferghal pounces on me.

Of course, I do want to have a talk with him, but not necessarily in company with the Major, or Valerie, who is hovering near the reception desk.

And I'm thinking that before I talk to anyone else at all, it would be a good idea to sit down and speir out all the meanings hidden behind the things Senga and Aileen have said just now. Because who knows? It might turn out that after I've thought it all through, I'd be asking Fer-ghal something different...

But before I can say a word, Ferghal takes Lianna's passport out of his pocket and hands it to me. It never occurred to me that Ferghal would have Lianna's passport. Why did he take it? Why does he still have it? Why is he giving it to me?

"Ferghal, why didn't you give Lianna's passport to Inspector Cler-mont?"

"I didn't have it, not then."

"Well, you've got it now, and why – " He just grins at me, the cheeky wee spalpeen, and interrupts.

"Drinkies before any more questions." And he takes my arm to lead me into the bar. But right then I catch sight of the clock above the reception desk. It's five to four.

The Major will be turning up any minute.

"Hold on a sec." I break away and march over to reception.

"When Major Peverel arrives" and at the sound of his name, the Major puffs up from one of the lobby chairs, blowing like a walrus.

"Ah, m'dear, here I am. What's this young scoundrel been up to, eh?" and he jabs Ferghal in the ribs with his cane.

And I would be astonished at the way he's moved in the blink of an eye from the lobby chair to within striking distance of poor Ferghal, only I'm not, because this time I was looking at the Major when he made his move, and I see that he isn't really a decrepit old man at all.

Why does he like to pretend that he is? He seems to want everyone to think that he's ancient and wobbly, but he's quite nimble – and now that I come to think about it, if he was stationed here during the war, and then he was demobbed with the rank of major, it's quite likely that he was young when he was in Paris, much more likely than not.

Why, he may not be much more than 50ish, not old at all really.

The Major has got a lot of explaining to do. But there isn't time to go into any of that now. I'm going to see to it that he and I have a long talk later, though.

We go into the bar to talk. Valerie tags along too.

I'd rather have talked to Ferghal alone, but I am not going to be deterred by having the pack of them around me. One odd thing is going to get explained, at least. How did Ferghal get Lianna's passport? He's at the bar now, getting in the drinks, and turns to ask what I'd like.

"Te- café au lait, please."

The Major takes a small beer, and Ferghal gets a bottle of red wine to share with Valerie. He waves the wine bottle at her, pointing to the label, mutely asking her if it's the kind of wine she likes – and she gets a most peculiar look on her face.

It's almost as if she doesn't want to drink with him, but it can't be that, they're friends.

Yet it's upsetting her to see him waving that bottle. Another oddity. Oh, well, maybe it's bad for the wine if you wave the bottle about – the French are obsessed with the conditions under which wine is stored and drunk.

Valerie nods at Ferghal – it's the right kind of wine – and turns her head away, muttering. I catch a few words. "My father comes to Paris after all these years and *he* (the words fade) **silly fireworks** (the words fade)"

It seems like forever before we're all sitting around a tiny bar table with our drinks and I can get back to the point.

"All right, Ferghal, why didn't you give Lianna's passport to Inspector Clermont?"

"I didn't have it, not then." He's grinning, thoroughly enjoying being the centre of attention, and I remember how full of himself he was on the train. It's all a game to him.

Well, it's certainly not a game to me. Poor Lianna locked up in a Paris pokey, and all because this imbecile didn't tell the Inspector the full story when he was questioned.

But then I think back to how imperious Inspector Clermont was. Maybe Ferghal didn't get a chance to tell the Inspector the full story. And it's obvious looking at him that he thinks he's done something very clever, so probably the quickest way to get to the bottom of it all is just to let him tell the three of us all about how clever he's been.

He's a pest, but I smile at him and nod encouragingly, so he'll start talking. Not that he needs any encouragement.

Well, he clutters up his story with a lot of irrelevant rubbish about what he had for his supper and why he decided to go out to a casino instead of sitting down with a good book like any sensible person would, but eventually he gets to where he's passing the Hôtel Albert on his way to the casino down the street, and out sallies Lianna for a breath of fresh air.

They both exclaim about their paths crossing again like that so soon, and then she says there are no seats in the lobby, so she's come out to see if she can find a café.

"Well," he says, "I told her 'There'll be no cafes with empty seats, macushla, not at this time on a Friday night in the heart of Paris. They're all of them crammed full by eight. And not the best place for a young lady on her own, either. Better come with me to the casino, where this early on there's plenty of seats to be had, and the darling place only a step down the road.' "

So far, this matches what Lianna told me. Just after eight-thirty she went out to get a breath of fresh air, Ferghal happened to be passing – and she saw no harm in accepting his invitation. After all, she had the brass neck to say, it's not like he's a stranger, they've been introduced by Valerie, and he'd given her his card with the promise to take her and me sightseeing if she likes. As Lianna was saying all that her hangdog face made it clear as crystal she knew fine and well what I'd have had to say about it if I'd been there.

"And why didn't you tell Inspector Clermont this, Ferghal?"

He's all injured innocence. "Sure an' I did, Màiri. I told the man the whole story, just like I'm telling it to you now." He drinks his wine, waiting to be asked to go on.

The Major barks, "Get on with it, man."

Well, Ferghal can interpret that as an invitation or an order, up to him. He shrugs.

"Not much more to tell, Major. When we got to the casino, they wouldn't let Lianna in, not even as my guest, without her passport. It's some regulation. Typical Frenchie double-think. If she's followed the regulation to hand in her passport at the hotel, how will she still have it to hand in according to regulations at the casino?" He stops and has another drink.

But you get your passport back again. Ferghal lives in Paris. How does he not know that you get your passport back again after the police have inspected it?

Màiri's Mental Note: Be careful of Ferghal. He may be a liar. Something's fishy here...

I lean towards him. "Yes, but she got in somehow, didn't she Ferghal?"

"Ah weeell, yes and no. There's a Ladies Room in the lobby and a sort of cloakroom with a couple of chairs. It's not part of the casino proper, so I said Lianna should go and get herself a seat over there while I sorted it out, and she did. But I couldn't sort it out. And when I went to fetch her, she'd gone."

The Major barks at Ferghal "Passport" meaning Ferghal should tell us how he got hold of it.

I stand up. The Major, being old school, immediately rises also, almost by reflex. Ferghal, being practically a card-carrying member of the classless society, stays seated.

The Major glares down at him with still deeper disapproval. "Young man! A lady has risen!" Ferghal doesn't even get it, so then I know that for all his airs, he wasn't born a toff.

I lay a soothing hand on the Major's arm. "Ellis, won't you please stay and entertain Valerie? I want Ferghal to take me to this casino. We won't be long."

Put like that, the Major has to sit down again. He can't possibly come with us. That would be rude to Valerie. A gentleman is never rude, except on purpose.

Ferghal is still seated, so I grab his ear and twist. "Come along, ma braw laddie. I've taken a notion to see this not-quite-casino cloakroom."

Ferghal gets up, since it's that or lose his ear, and we head out to the casino.

Aileen doesn't feel that she really got through to Harry, for all that she talked his ear off. It's all very well for him, living off the fat of the land with that casino raking in more money than you can count. He should remember his roots.

Her mammy had been good to him when he was a scabby-knee'd wean, and for that matter she had been good to him too, pulling him out of fights and sharing her play piece with him most days.

If not for free school dinners and her mammy giving him his tea as often as not and all those play pieces she'd shared with him, he'd likely have starved what with that druggie mother of his aye off in Cloud Cuckoo Land and him no fitting in at all at school, what with his daftie stories about how much better everything was in Durham than in Glasgow.

Her friends had been glad to see the back of him when his mammy got put into the hospital and his daddy came to fetch him back to Durham, but *she'd* stayed in touch, and lied for him that weekend they'd spent together in Scarborough when the poliss came for him.

He'd have done time then, if not for her. And when he did do time later, she'd been there for him in his trouble. He should remember that and help her in her trouble now.

Yes, that rat of a taxman is dead and gone – but that's not enough to save her, not on its own.

She'd never meant to cheat on her taxes. It was just she hadn't ever had any money except for her wages, where they take the taxes first and give you the rest, and so she hadn't known she needed to file a tax return saying her granny had left her a wee bit of money.

And by the time she found out about the tax that was due, she'd spent what she had.

The tax wasn't all that much, really, she could probably have managed just the tax somehow, but that slimeball Charlie Stout had gone and written all those lies into the tax records about her doing it on purpose.

She'll never be able to pay all the penalties and fines. Harry needs to remember how much he owes her and help her out. He's got people who understand these things. He needs to get one of them to go into the tax records and take out everything Stout said about her.

Then there will be just the tax due, and she can pay that somehow.

I ask Ferghal, as we're coming up to the casino door, which genuinely is a mere step down the road from our *pension*, "How did you come to have Lianna's passport, Ferghal?"

"Well, when Lianna and me went there yesterday, as the luck chances, the fella on duty at the entrance was a sort of a pal of mine. He's on the same shift today, two until ten. The passport got handed in just before he came on duty, and because he remembered Lianna came in with me, he gave it to me to give to her instead of holding it in Lost Property for the gendarmes."

Curiouser and curiouser. Who had Lianna's passport yesterday? How did they get it? Why do they want to be rid of it today? And how come Ferghal's inside a casino nattering away with his pal before it's even turned four in the afternoon? Doesn't he ever work?

We go in, and while Ferghal is explaining to his friend the entrance attendant that I only want to have a quick look at the cloakroom seating, I'm into the Ladies. But I can't see any powder room attendant, which is surprising in a place like this.

Just as Lianna had said, there's a mirrored seating area for applying your make-up with a wee counter to put your lipstick and stuff on. That's where she sat down and fell asleep.

She came to with her head on the counter – and no idea whether she'd been out cold for just seconds or for hours. Oh, if only there'd been a powder room attendant to alibi her!

But maybe there was a powder room attendant here yesterday. Or maybe one of the casino's lady members came in and saw her.

I send up a silent prayer. *Dear Father in Heaven, please let someone have seen her. Please! I'll never be late for the Mass again.*

Ferghal and me spend so long in the casino trying to find someone who has seen Lianna that we nearly miss the tour group's outing to the Eiffel Tower.

But Ferghal happens to see Valerie passing the casino's open doorway with the Major at her side and the City Break tourists crowding her like a gaggle of little ducklings all coorying in around their mother, so we rush out in time to catch up with them before they're lost to sight.

We catch a bus to the Eiffel Tower. Valerie has week-long full bus passes for all of us as part of our tour package. Ferghal, being resident in Paris, has one of his own. The bus ride takes us more than twenty-five minutes.

I whip out my notebook as we come up to the Tower entrance and scribble down a quick aide-memoire.

Màiri's Note: Update all Time-frame Notes. Lots of wrong times + 25 min bus to Tower.

As we're queuing up to get in the lift to the top, Valerie realises that we're a ticket short.

For once, Yvonne departs from her profound calm, saying a bit hysterically that she wants to take her Charlie's ticket and lay it in his grave. Valerie has to tell her, as tactfully as she can, that Mr Stout had taken his own ticket from her the previous night.

Yvonne bursts into tears, and Valerie is very good with her, very soothing, and after a bit of a cry (which probably did her good, she's been too calm) Yvonne starts wiping her eyes.

So then Valerie returns to the ticket issue. Lianna's ticket is a spare, but we have brought two extras, Ferghal and the Major. I point out that Ferghal is my guest, and since I invited him, I'll go and get an extra ticket.

Ferghal makes no demur so I turn aside to the ticket booth, and of course the Major peels off with me because he's too much of a gentleman to let any lady stand in any queue unescorted whilst he's on hand to look after her. It's sweet and charming and as irritating as all-get-out.

We're in the classless '70s, not the 1900s.

Why, I've friends who don't even hold swing doors open for me anymore (mind, they say things like "You see I am not holding this door open…" or "I am not waiting for you to go through this door first…" "…because I respect you as an equal", which is even more irritating in its own way. I always say I won't feel disrespected if they hold the door open, but they pay me no heed.)

The reason I'm in the ticket queue, of course, is to see if anyone remembers anything about when Valerie came for the group's tickets last night – and the Major doesn't merely beat me to the draw, he takes over completely.

"Ah" he begins and breaks into fast and voluble French, using a lot of gestures. I don't understand a word.

The three people in the ticket booth and office respond instantly. They break into even faster and more excitable speech than the Major did, all talking together, with huge movements of their hands. In fact, there's so much waving of hands going on that I can get the gist of what they're saying even though I don't understand the words.

When Valerie came last night, she was accompanied by a man. But she didn't pick up the tickets, not then. She went away with the man, and later she came back on her own.

When she came, it was nearly time for them to close up. They had the window half down, but of course for her they opened it again, and gave her the group's tickets, and then closed up.

I'm stunned. The ticket office doesn't close until ten o'clock.

Can it be that *Valerie*, who seems so kind-hearted, is really the killer?

But then the Major whips out Polaroid photos (taken from the *dossier* files) of Charlie Stout and Mr Brown and Ferghal and Jimmy and Rhys and lays them all in a row.

The ticket people all smile at me, fondly imagining that they are speaking English. "Yes, yes, 'arree, eet ees 'arreee," they say, pointing to the photo of Mr Harry Brown, who had stayed at home all night from the moment the train got in, according to his wife...

And they call him by his first name. They must know him well. What reason does he have to come here often enough that the ticket people know him well?

Màiri's Mental Note: What business takes Mr Brown to the Eiffel Tower so frequently?

We don't go up the Tower. We go back to the Major's hotel instead, for some soothing tea and a good solid dinner, which by now I badly need!

It has been a topsy-turvy day, one stunning discovery after another, and my brain is bursting with it all; in fact, I have quite a bad headache. But in spite of my headache, I'm brim full of curiosity. It feels like the more I learn, the more unanswered questions there are.

After Dinner Mints

Chapter 8 After Dinner Mints

7:10 p.m. Saturday, 15th August, 1970

Hôtel Marquis, Rue Greneta, Paris, France

I'm very tired. It's been a long, hectic day.

"You're looking a little peaky, m'dear," says the Major, as he puts his hand behind my left shoulder to guide me into his hotel's dining room. "Let's get some tiffin first and then compare notes."

And because I *am* tired – and let's face it, because I'm an English teacher – I recognise that he's definitely playing a part. Tiffin isn't a word that was widely used by officers in the war, and it's not a word in common English use. It's a colonial word, and the Major has given no indication that he served in the Colonies (which practically don't exist anymore anyway).

I'm worn out and I have a headache, so I'm just a little bit vexed.

It's not quite good manners (I'm his guest, after all) but nonetheless, I decide to let him know that I know.

"Jolly good, and let's have a stingah before our tiffin." Stingah is another colonial word. It means a drink with a lot of whiskey in it. Or gin, but I think it's said a slightly different way when it's gin.

"Rumbled, eh?" And the Major gives me a rather beautiful smile. "Mind you, a large Scotch would do you good right now, old girl. Or would you rather have aspirin?"

"Aspirin, please, Ellis. And food sounds like heaven."

So we go into the dining room in a good temper with each other and I get my aspirin and the headache slowly retreats. Dinner is stunning. Not as good as our Morag's cooking, of course, no one can cook like Morag – but this isn't "cooking" exactly. Cooking is too simple a word for it. This is something only a kitchen staff of dozens could produce.

I'd rather have Morag's trifle than *Crepes Suzette*, of course, but have you ever eaten *Crepes Suzette*? It's a taste bomb exploding in your mouth. And that was dessert, when my taste buds were already tingling after the first three incredible courses.

Morag's Scotch Broth is the tastiest thing to come home to on a cold winter day that you can ever imagine! But this isn't a cold day, it's much too hot, and so the cold soup they served us was lovely. Vichyssoise it's called. It's made from potatoes and leeks. Plenty of potatoes and leeks in Glasgow. I wonder could Morag maybe find a recipe... but who ever heard of a cold soup? No one I've spoken to, that's certain.

We have wonderful fish in Glasgow, the best haddock in the world! Our own lovely sweet wee haddock, that ye cannae get anywhere else. You want to taste what they call haddock in Whitby, that's all I can say, and then come to Glasgow and walk into any chippie, and you'll wonder why they call Fish & Chips an **English** meal.

But for our dinner, they gave us sea bass in a sauce that was another taste explosion, and tiny pieces of vegetable the size of my thumbnail, all different, and all of it very good.

And tiny lamb cutlets broiled to perfection and *pommes frites*, which are kind of like wee thin chips, only not really. They make *frites* at our hotel too, but not nearly so good as these.

It was a marvellous dinner, and as far as I'm concerned, the Major can be the King of Persia in disguise and I wouldn't say a word, no' when I'm getting fed like that!

After dinner we go through to that beautiful sitting room for some more marvellous tea.

I haven't said a word yet about any of the things I want to know about the Major, because that's not what matters. Lianna is banged up in a French pokey and I need to give everything I've got to the task of getting her out. The Major's antics are not of overpowering interest to me when weighted in that scale. He's helping the freedom fight, that's all that counts now.

Plenty of time later to corner him and get the truth out of him.

So instead of demanding answers from him, I show the Major all the notes I made during this very long day.

Màiri's Note 1: Check the time Tax Charlie left Hôtel Albert

I tell the Major the saga of Senga's specs. "The times in the dossier are definitely wrong."

He frowns. "Then Stout couldn't have been at the Eiffel Tower at nine o'clock. The skunk must have left Hôtel Albert just after a quarter to nine, which means he couldn't have arrived any earlier than a quarter past."

Reminded of his vendetta against Stout, I'm tempted to ask why, but I control the impulse.

The Major reaches for a piece of hotel notepaper, and draws a new grid. He puts the times for Stout leaving the hotel and arriving at the Tower in the proper boxes. No other times yet!

	8:45 p.m.	9 p.m.	9:15 p.m.
Charlie Stout	leaves Hôtel	on BUS to Tower	Eiffel Tower

Then he sits back, stroking his moustache. "We know Stout must have travelled there by bus; he couldn't have reached the Tower by foot in less than an hour."

I'm not so sure. "Someone might have taken him there by car. In fact, I mind Valerie said to me that she drove him there. Or no, wait a bit, she didn't say that, not exactly, but she drove there herself, and I think that she took him with her."

"A thought. Distinctly a thought. Let's see, who has a car?"

Suspects:

Ferghal Reilly   Harry Brown   Valerie

But again, I'm not so sure that's right. Some thought is knocking at the back of my mind. But I can't quite remember what. Did I make a note of it? I glance through my notes.

So then I tell the Major about my conversation with Aileen; how fierce she is against Stout. And she knows Harry Brown. It could have been the two of them working together.

Or she could have sneaked out of their room; Senga is so short-sighted she would have believed a bolster in the bedclothes was Aileen.

The Major adds Aileen to his list.

Suspects:

Ferghal Reilly   Harry Brown   Valerie   Aileen

He coughs. "Let's see. Assume everyone is lying. Who else could the killer be?"

"It couldn't be Mrs Stout. She was with me during the whole of the murder time frame and she doesn't know anyone in Paris."

"She might be lying about not knowing anyone." But I notice that the Major doesn't add her to his suspects list. "There are those two young men. They alibi each other. So one of them might be the killer. Or both."

I shake my head. "They couldn't have arrived at the Tower in time. They were in the lobby until nine and a quarter past nine."

"Well, m'dear, how do we know the exact time of death? We relied on what Valerie said. And now we know that she was mistaken in the times at best, and probably she was lying in her teeth."

I'm shaken by his reasoning. I can't think of Valerie as a killer, or even as an accomplice to the killer, but what the Major says is true...

He takes a new sheet of paper and writes all the names down. "Narrowed it down to six suspects, m'dear." And he sounds *cheerful* about it!

Suspects:

Ferghal Reilly	Harry Brown	Valerie	Aileen	Jimmy Orville	Rhys 1

And then I remember that it makes no difference. I can prove that several witnesses have lied to Inspector Clermont, and that means the gendarmes will have to let Lianna go.

What do I care who killed Charlie Stout?

I just want Lianna back where she belongs.

However, I know lots of things that will help Ellis in his ongoing search for the murderer, although I don't know why he should care who did it either. So I tell him what I've noticed.

"Well, we have a starting point. Harry Brown seems to be at the centre of things. He was at the Tower with Valerie at the right time to murder Stout. And now I come to think about it, Valerie told me she doesn't know him. But she must know him if she was with him when she went to the ticket office. He lied about his whereabouts and he got his wife to lie for him too." I take another sip of tea and nibble on one of the chocolate mints they brought us.

"And Brown also has some kind of connection to Aileen. She was talking to him quite near the murder time frame window. And she lied about it. She says she just fell into conversation with Harry Brown and doesn't know him – but I could see that was a lie. He's getting a lot of people to lie for him... I wonder how?" These are really good mints. I take another.

"And that's not all. Aileen hates Tax Charlie. To be so bitter against him she must have some reason. Her reason may have something to do with Brown." I finish the mint and I'm about to take another when I see they're all gone. Have I really eaten six mints?

I sigh, and tell Ellis about another clue.

"And then this afternoon I saw Ferghal talking to Brown at the casino. It could all just be a coincidence, but it looks like a spider's web with Brown at the centre."

I sip some more tea. "We have an easy way to clear Ferghal too, if he's not the killer. He says that he was in the casino during the murder time frame window. He spends a lot of time in that casino. Lots of people know him. If he was there, it should be easy enough to find a lot of people who saw him and provide an overlapping time layer to establish that he was there."

The Major nods. "Yes, m'dear, good point. And if he wasn't there, a complete lack of people who saw him would be a strong indicator. Not definitive, of course."

"And something very curious happened today. Lianna's passport suddenly turned up at the casino. But she didn't have it with her when she went to the casino. How did it get there?"

I've been looking across at Ellis as I'm sipping my tea – and I swear I nearly abandoned my policy of not questioning him. Because when I was telling him about Lianna's passport, his whole body stiffened. For a second, he looked exactly like a pointer dog on the scent.

But I keep my focus on the important stuff. *Let's get Lianna out first, **then** I'll discover the Major's secrets.* Which is very strong-minded of me, because I'm dying of curiosity.

I glance down at my notes again.

Màiri's Note 3: Check Aileen's *dossier* notes. Find out her connection to Tax Charlie

"Let's look through Aileen's *dossier* file again and see if anything in there can tell us why she hates Tax Charlie."

But there's nothing in Aileen's file that helps us. Not only are the *dossier* files of no help there, but the questions in my last note also remain unanswered.

Màiri's Note 4: Why is Aileen lying about Brown? Did they conspire together to kill?

There is nothing I can see to do that will help us find out the answers...

And the neat little grid of times and places we had only yesterday is all torn up. The new grid is all over the place.

Murder Time frame based on times recorded in *dossier*

	9 p.m.	9:15 p.m.	9:30 p.m.	9:43 p.m.
Major Peverel	British Embassy	leaves 11 p.m.		
Harry Brown	in casino	Eiffel Tower	Tower	Eiffel Tower
Ferghal Reilly	in casino	Eiffel Tower	Tower	Eiffel Tower
Valerie	at Eiffel Tower	Eiffel Tower	Tower	Eiffel Tower
Aileen & Senga Jimmy Orville	in their room check in ends	in his room?	in his room?	all night?
Rhys Williams Màiri	Checks In hotel queue	check in ends Checks In	visits JO? dining	in bed?? dining
Lianna	leaves 8:50 p.m. BUS/car to	at casino, asleep powder room: leaves 10:14		
Charlie Stout	Tower	Eiffel Tower	?	?
Yvonne Stout	hotel queue	hotel queue	Checks In	dining

It's getting late now and the Major insists on walking me back to the Hôtel Albert.

When I see how crowded and noisy the streets of Paris are at this time on a Saturday night, I'm glad he did insist.

Sometimes it's nice for a girl to know a man wants to protect her. I feel grateful to the Major. Perhaps there's something to be said for the outmoded gallantry of the 1900s after all.

We part at the entrance to my *pension*.

"By the way, dear girl, I hope I didn't come across as too much of an old fuddy-duddy today. Had to look like a fatuous chump from the 1900s, y'know. Pull the wool over their eyes. Couldn't let anyone suspect we were playing a double game."

Ellis pauses, and I can see he's wondering how best to say something that's important to him; that my opinion about whatever's on his mind at this moment actually matters to him – he's searching for the right words.

"But I want you to know, Màiri, that I respect you as an equal."

Never on
a Sunday

Chapter 9 Never On A Sunday

11:20 p.m. Saturday, 15th August, 1970

Tristan Toussaint's Home, Paris, France

Tristan Toussaint comes reluctantly into his kitchen, drawn by the insistent ringing of the Hotline set up for him when the joint operation began.

"Hello?" No point in speaking anything but English, not on this telephone line.

"Good evening, my friend. Let's meet for a drink."

"No, no, my dear confrère. This late, I drink only with my wife. And tomorrow is Sunday. You know that I do not work on Sundays. We will meet on Monday morning, in my office."

"You've worked with me on a Sunday before now, Tristan."

"But yes, mon vieux. In the long ago days when we were young. Now a national department rests on my head. Which needs sleep, mon ami. It is not so young a head as once."

"Her passport has turned up. In that place."

"Ah"

"Your men did spot those thugs at Orly? They are being tailed?"

"How can you ask?"

"How do you want me to play it now?"

"Perhaps, for her friend's safety – "

"She's safe. I'm with her most of the time. Your people are watching her too."

"So. Do you have enough, camarade, to bring them all in?"

"Not yet."

"Then we must continue."

"We need to work out a new plan."

"On Monday, Ellis. Bon nuit.

I feel weird when I wake up in the room on my own, with Lianna's bed lying there empty. But I am feeling very happy now that I have the ammunition to make the Sûreté free her.

Firstly, her passport has been found. In deeply suspicious circumstances, granted. But I have no intention of telling the gendarmes all the circumstances.

I shall simply say that the day we arrived (as they know themselves from the *dossier*) Lianna went out before she had surrendered her passport to the hotel safe, to a casino, and it had got lost; next day the casino found her passport, and it was given to me to give to the Sûreté.

The truth if not all of the truth.

Of course, if you're being picky, it's what mum calls "living a lie" but I am not about to get picky when my best friend is rotting in a French holding cell.

Secondly, we have incontrovertible proof that the times in the *dossier* are all a-kilter. I have the two sets of times and places right there in my notebook ready to show them.

Thirdly, lots of witnesses had lied to Inspector Clermont, and their lies had not been noticed. An obvious reason to hold a new hearing and find out what really happened.

And all of that had been discovered in just one day! What a whirlwind investigation...

I probably won't be able to get Lianna freed today, because it's Sunday. Inspector Toussaint had been really clear about the need for a second *dossier* hearing before Lianna can be freed and there isn't going to be a second hearing on a Sunday, obviously.

But I can go and see her and share the good news with her. Right after Mass.

So I get out of bed to get ready for church and I realise that there's been so much going on from the moment we arrived at Gare du Nord that I haven't even begun to unpack yet.

All my dresses are creased from being in my suitcase too long, with my laundry bag holding the dirty clothes I'd worn in London lumped in on top. That's what comes of hurried packing.

I wonder if I can borrow an iron from the hotel? I can't go to Mass in a dress that's creased!

It takes me a few minutes to get the clerk at reception to understand, but then he says a maid will bring me an iron and I go back to the room. While I'm waiting, I stuff all the clothes I've worn here into my laundry bag and hang it in the washroom.

The iron still hasn't arrived, so I begin to unpack.

After I've hung up four dresses, I find a sponge bag tucked in just under them. It isn't my sponge bag; it's a very classy toiletries bag. I wonder if when we packed up in our Bayswater B&B Lianna had accidentally put her washing things into my suitcase? It's just the sort of really beautiful travel accessory that Lianna would buy.

But surely, tired though we had been on Friday night, Lianna had brushed her teeth before climbing into bed?

I go back into the little washroom beside our room (we share the washroom with another room, but no one is occupying that room just now, so we have it to ourselves) so as to check, and sure enough, Lianna's sponge bag is sitting on a shelf above the basin.

It's a lovely glossy striped one that I remember now I saw her take into the washroom with her when we were staying at our Bayswater B&B.

So where did this super-ritzy toiletries bag come from? How did it get into my suitcase?

It isn't mine and it isn't Lianna's... but I'm not about to worry my head over someone else's sponge bag when I need to get ready for Mass.

The maid arrives with the iron and I ask her to put the bag into Lost Property. But we have a communication breakdown. So, in the end, I just lay it on my bed while I iron my dress so's I can get ready for church.

When I'm ready, I take the fancy bag downstairs with me as well as my huge brass key fob and lay them both on the reception desk.

But again, there seems to be some difficulty in getting across the concept of a Lost Property office, and I don't want to risk being late for the Mass, so after a bit of to-ing and fro-ing I ask the clerk to put the beautiful toiletries bag into the hotel's safe instead.

I wait until I see him do it before leaving for the early Mass at the Basilique du Sacré-Cœur.

There's probably a nearer church, but the Sacred Heart Basilica is a famous tourist sight, and I have always had a deep devotion to the Sacred Heart.

After the unexpected way in which my prayer had been answered yesterday (because all I wanted was for Lianna to be freed and now she will be) I'm certainly not going to complain about taking half an hour's bus ride so as to hear the Mass.

I didn't know before I got there, but they have Perpetual Exposition of the Blessed Sacrament at the Basilica. I asked a Verger when the Adoration began. It was nearly *85 years* ago.

Think of it! In our parish, we're as devout as most – more devout than many. And we've never had an Adoration of the Blessed Sacrament that lasted longer than five days. Hard enough to get people to agree to take an Hour's Prayer Time at 2 a.m., 3 a.m., 4 a.m. for as long as five days.

But here in Paris, they have been worshipping the Blessed Sacrament around the clock for just short of 85 years...

You know that wonderful feeling of peace in Glasgow Cathedral, in any church that's open all day and people come to pray and all that prayer seeps into the walls?

You can't imagine the feeling of peace in the Basilique du Sacré-Cœur. It took my breath.

Being in the Basilica is an indescribable experience. If you are ever in Paris, you should be sure to visit and feel all that peace and love yourself. It's beautiful.

The building itself is a little too square and elaborate for my taste, but it's considered to be an architectural triumph.

I'm there before the Mass starts, in plenty of time to light a candle in thanksgiving. Then I kneel before the Monstrance, and gazing up at the Host, I thank Our Blessed Lord for having shown me the right questions to ask so that now Lianna will be safe.

A fter Mass, I pop into a nearby café and have a huge *café complet,* which is the French name for a breakfast without porridge or any other hot food. But they certainly give you a lot of it so I'm not complaining. When I'm paying the bill, I see that I have accidentally ordered and eaten a breakfast for two people. What a reddie! I must bring Lianna here for *café complet,* so we can laugh together about what a greedy-guts I've been.

Very soon me and Lianna will be racketing all over Paris, trying to cram in all the best sights and buy all the prettiest clothes and eat all the most delicious meals before we have to board the train to Istanbul on Friday morning. I head for the police station.

The gendarmes on duty log in Lianna's passport. They don't make any difficulty about giving us time together. They put us into quite a pleasant room and send in coffee. We're so happy.

I'm up with the lark on Monday morning, my heart singing. Today is a working day, so they can hold a second *dossier* hearing.

At the police station, they tell me Inspector Toussaint isn't there. I'm glad he's having some time with his family. Then I realise I don't know if he has a family. I hope that he's having a good day off anyway.

They send me to Inspector Clermont. The Inspector is very polite. But he refuses point blank to schedule a second *dossier* hearing. Even after I show him my notebook.

The Inspector looks at it all very carefully. He understands everything I'm showing him. He compliments me on the hard work I have done establishing all this. He is enchanted with my powers of observation. He says nice things about my deductive reasoning. He says Lianna is lucky to have a friend like me who is determined to show her innocence. And then he refuses to schedule a second *dossier* hearing.

"But you *know* she didn't do it." I wail.

"Ah, no, Miss Maguire. This is precisely what I do not know. It is for the magistrate to know. I gather the facts for the magistrate and he decides. Is it impossible that Miss Stuart does this? Is it unlikely? Is it likely? These are decisions for a court. What you have made clear, is that many people have not been truthful. This is not unusual. It changes nothing."

He means what he says. He explains.

From the standpoint of the French justice system, the truth gets established at a trial.

Charlie Stout was killed at the Eiffel Tower. That is a fact. It is now known (the Inspector gives me a little bow) that he could not have been killed any earlier than 9:30 p.m. He was dead by 10:30 p.m. These are facts.

People often lie. This is well known.

Miss Stuart was asleep in the casino entrance Ladies Room from 8:50 p.m. until 10:10 p.m. This is not a fact, it is what she says. It is possible that she was at the Eiffel Tower killing Charlie Stout at 9:30 p.m. If so, she could still have been back at Hôtel Albert by 10:15 p.m.

If a witness comes forward to say that she is seen asleep in the casino entrance Ladies Room at any time between 9:05 p.m. and 10:05 p.m. that is very good for Miss Stuart; but it is still not a fact, it is only what Miss Stuart says and what another person says, which to a certain extent corroborates what Miss Stuart says.

Certainly, if that happened, he would call for an early magistrate's hearing and the magistrate would decide. If two people came forward, the magistrate would almost certainly decide that what Miss Stuart says is true, especially since no one who could have seen her has a motive to lie that they have seen her. If even one person came forward, the magistrate would be very likely to decide that Miss Stuart could not have been at the Eiffel Tower when Mr Stout was killed; she would most probably be freed.

But there is no reason to hold a second *dossier* hearing, because no new facts which have any bearing on whether she killed Charlie Stout or not have been brought to light.

I'm shattered, but I can't argue against what he says. I ask sadly if I may see Lianna...

E llis Peverel is waiting to confer with the head of Direction générale de la sécurité extérieure when 9:00 a.m. rolls around. He knows that he is in a uniquely privileged position.

Of course, their joint op with Scotland Yard is important to the Sûreté. Italian Interpol's stake in the outcome lends him extra authority. And naturally French national security will go to great lengths to prevent bombs exploding in the middle of Paris. So when a lunatic may have smuggled a Senegalese bomb into Paris, his high standing within ATJF gives him gravitas.

But even so, he knows that the man at the top would not spend so much time listening to his theories, or give him carte blanche to run this op his own way – let alone follow his lead – if not for the war years they had spent in the Resistance together.

Tristan trusts him.

I've broken the terrible news to Lianna. I don't know how I managed to force the words out.

It's after 11 o'clock by now, and I realise that I must call Lianna's family to let them know what has happened. But then it strikes me that I don't have a telephone number for her parents or for any of her brothers. I sink down on a bench by the door and I just can't help crying.

Lianna's family are bound to blame me for taking her away from them and letting this awful thing happen to her. And then not even telling them. I don't know what to do.

And I know that I must stop crying and be strong for Lianna but I can't seem to be strong for her right now. I fish for my hankie but I can't find it, and I don't even care that I'm in public and everyone can see me crying. I have never felt so helpless. Then a hand picks up mine and puts a big hankie into it. I put my whole face into the hankie and sob.

Someone sinks onto the bench beside me and puts an arm around me. "There, there, old girl, get it all out, that's right." and Ellis gathers me into his chest and pats my back and just as I'm beginning to recover enough to feel embarrassed, he lets go of me and gives me a new hankie. "Have you had anything to eat today?"

I'm sobbing a bit less now and I manage to shake my head. I hadn't had any breakfast at the hotel, because I had idiotically thought that I would have *café complet* sent in for Lianna and me to share while we waited together for the hearing.

Of course, neither of us had any heart to eat once I'd told her there would be no hearing today. And I am in no mood to eat now either, only a monster could think of food at a time like this, and I get angry enough with the Major to stop crying altogether.

"This is no time to be fussing over food."

"Oh, but it is, old girl, must keep your strength up, can't think clearly on an empty stomach. Tell Uncle Ellis what the trouble is."

Bit by bit I get the story out.

"So what's your priority, Màiri? Telling Lianna's family she's in trouble or finding a way to get her out of trouble?"

I can't make any sense of that. "What do you mean?"

"I mean if your friend had wanted her family to know she would have told them. She knows her mother's telephone number. She knows that the police would have given her a telephone if she'd asked. The Sûreté always play a straight bat. I'll be most surprised if they didn't *offer* her use of a phone. So if your friend isn't calling her family, Màiri, it's because she's relying on you to help her. Are you going to let her down?"

How dare he! I can't remember when I was last so angry. How dare he sit there and preach at me! It isn't his friend who was led away in handcuffs and locked up in a foreign prison. How *dare* he accuse me of not wanting to help Lianna, when I'd do anything to see her go free.

"That's the ticket." He stands up and hauls me to my feet. "Let's get you an omelette. You'll see things differently when you've eaten."

Harry Brown doesn't know Major Ellis Peverel but they are in complete agreement about the importance of fuelling the inner man. He munches on a giant club sandwich whilst his team goes into action. A true leader knows when to delegate.

When his lads are done, Ferghal Reilly's good looks are messed up, but there's no permanent damage done, except maybe a broken nose. Maybe not. Hard to tell right now.

They've done a good job. Brown thinks complacently *Just as I told them. Not hurt the stupid git much yet, because I might need him to be able to walk, but hurt him enough so he knows that real pain is on the cards if he doesn't straighten up fast. Good lads.*

"Alright me boyo, let's take it from the top. You got on the train at Le Havre, right?"

Ferghal swallows a couple of times and manages to croak out "Yes, boss"

"And you found the woman whose luggage Magatte had targeted on the boat, and got Valerie to introduce you to her, right?"

"Yes, boss"

"And you waited your moment and got hold of her passport for Magatte to use crossing the border into Italy, right?"

"Yes, boss"

"And she had no idea you'd done that?"

Ferghal shakes his head, which is a mistake, the blood starts flowing again. "Not a clue." He mops at his nose with the back of his hand.

"And while she was passed out in the Ladies Room, you got her keys"

Ferghal nods.

"And went to her hotel to fetch the detonator –"

"Yes, boss"

"Now this is what I don't understand, my lad. Why did you swipe her keys?"

"She'd locked the case"

"And you knew that how?"

"I told you, boss. As soon as the bellboy got their luggage. I went to get the detonator but the case was locked." Ferghal's wiping at his nose with both hands now.

"So?"

"So I let him put it in the room and half inched a room key off him."

"Why didn't you break the case open?"

"Because you said to do it quietly, boss. You said not to let them know."

"That's right, you idiot. I said to do it quietly. And then you bring the Sûreté down on us like a rash!"

"Wasn't my fault. I didn't kill that taxman."

"No, you moron. What *you* did was a lot more damaging! Why didn't you slip her passport into her handbag when Magatte was done with it?"

"She was in clink."

"And every handbag she owns was in jail with her?"

Ferghal dabs at his nose.

"If you had to pull such a stupid theatrical stunt, why did you lead them *here?*"

"Where else was she likely to have lost her passport?"

"You brain-dead ape! If you'd done your job right, she'd never have known it was missing. Alright, maybe you're telling me the truth. That or the stupidest lie I've heard in a long time. ***What have you done with the detonator?***"

The intercom comes alive. "Harry, the gendarmes are here again."

Harry depresses the key. "I'll be right there."

He turns to the bouncers. "Don't let him pass out before I get back."

I am beginning to be a little uncomfortable that the Major is paying for so many of my meals. There doesn't seem to be much I can do about it.

I can't offer to pay in a public place. That would be shocking manners, terribly insulting to an old school type like Ellis.

I can't offer a return of hospitality; Morag's home-cooking is hundreds of miles away and the meals at Hôtel Albert don't bear comparison with the wonderful food at the Major's hotel.

I can't refuse to eat; that would be a worse insult than offering to pay.

I can't refuse to be in his company at mealtimes because the overriding priority is to find new facts which will force the Sûreté to let Lianna go, and facts seem to present themselves every minute of the day. Not that this has helped Lianna so far.

Perhaps there is some little gift that I can present him with, but what do you buy for the man who has everything? Because it is obvious that the Major is seriously rich.

Those pots of wonderful tea must cost a king's ransom to brew, here in the heart of a capital city that does not understand tea. How did he even teach them the way to do it?

Scrub the idea of buying a gift. I must *make* a present for him. What? I put the conundrum to the back of my mind, and there it bumps into a thought that coyly hides behind it. There was something I should have put into my notebook earlier and didn't. A clue. What was it?

I think back but nothing comes to me. It has something to do with me sitting in a café eating, because I'm sitting in a café eating now, and a tiny thought is fighting to make itself heard.

They call that a sense memory (a teacher learns a hundred ways to get knowledge branded into memory, how else are your pupils going to pass their exams?).

Something about where I am now is in some way similar to where I was when the elusive thought first came to me...

But Ellis is speaking. "So, m'dear, d'ye feel more the thing now?"

He beams at me when I admit that yes, the food has steadied me.

I dig out my notebook and when I look up again with the little book in my hand, I see that Ellis is still beaming, and suddenly I begin to wonder what he's getting out of all this.

Yes, it's lovely for me to have someone looking after me and feeding me and helping me to find some way to free Lianna – but why is the Major devoting himself to me like this?

Why has he helped me with the Sûreté? Why does he keep feeding me? Why does he spend so much time going through all the clues and papers with me? Why was he thrashing Tax Charlie? What does it matter to him whether Stout's killer is caught... and I realise I've hit it.

For some reason at present beyond my ken, Major Peverel (I had better stop thinking of him as Ellis) wants to catch Charlie Stout's killer. And he's using me as bait.

That's a totally irrational thought which came out of nowhere. And I know it's true. I don't know how or why, but for some reason I'm the goat tethered in the clearing, and the Major is the watchful hunter, waiting with loaded gun for the tiger to appear...

I immediately decide that he can whistle for his present. I'll not be wearing my fingers to the bone making a gift for this smarty-pants. If I'm his tethered goat, he has to feed me.

And to keep me safe from other predators, so that I'll still be a juicy mouthful when the tiger reaches the clearing.

The Plot Thickens

Chapter 10 The Plot Thickens

11:30 a.m. Monday, 17th August, 1970

Lucky 8 Casino, Rue du Faubourg Saint-Denis, Paris, France

Harry is geared up to handle any crisis, but it turns out that the interruption is nothing of any importance. Some missing form, which the office staff can handle. Harry thanks the bearers of bad tidings and insists that they take his contribution to whichever charity is flavour of the month.

Then he returns to his office and lights another Benson & Hedges. Ferghal eyes him warily.

"Now, you numbskull. Where's that detonator?"

"Wasn't my fault. I *told* you Magatte might speak to more than one woman."

"What are you rabbiting on about, you halfwit?"

"Magatte spoke to both of them, boss."

"WHO?"

"Lianna and Màiri."

"What has that got to do with the detonator?"

"I couldn't get it."

"WHY NOT?"

"I didn't have Màiri's suitcase keys, did I?"

Harry turns wearily to his bouncers.

"Get him cleaned up and go with him to Hôtel Albert. I don't care if you have to break down that woman's bedroom door and smash open every suitcase she's got, don't come back here without the detonator!"

"Yes, boss. What if she comes in while we're searching?"

"Then you'll have to silence her. Permanently. I don't need any more complications."

I'm silly to worry that I'm being used as bait. Nothing has really changed.

I still need to find new facts – or an alibi – so that Lianna can be freed. And whatever his reasons, the Major is helping me in a lot of ways.

There are suspects I haven't even spoken to yet, and time is slipping away fast.

"Ellis, we've got a lot of suspects. I think maybe you'd get more information from Mr Brown than I would, so how about I talk to Valerie, and then we can compare notes again? "

So the Major takes me back to Hôtel Albert and goes off to see Harry Brown.

Valerie is at the reception desk again. It turns out that Jimmy Orville isn't very well, and she's getting them to take some soup up to his room.

I suggest that we get some coffee. They serve it to us in the lobby.

To start the conversation going in the right direction, I ask Valerie how our tour group had liked being in the Eiffel Tower when they knew there had been a murder there – because when I thought about it later on, that was pretty creepy.

"Oh, no one seems to have thought about it. They were absorbed in the view of Paris, which is wonderful."

I'm wondering how to work the conversation around to all the lies she's told when Rhys Williams comes up and asks if he can join us for coffee, and of course Valerie introduces us.

So then I start to think about all the people Valerie introduces to each other, and I wonder about Harry Brown.

When I mention his name again, Valerie says, "Oh yes, Harry! Sorry, Màiri, my mind was somewhere else when we were talking on Saturday. I didn't think of Harry when you asked about "Mr Brown". Everyone knows Harry. And no one calls him Mr Brown."

Valerie seems quite willing to talk about Harry Brown but more interested in how Rhys and Jimmy are managing – which is her job, after all. She looks happy enough. There's nothing in her manner to indicate that Mr Brown means anything much to her, good or bad.

But a tiny voice in the back of my head is telling me that Valerie is upset with him, she's just hiding it well.

I look again at her smooth, serene face, and I don't know where that thought has come from. But there was something. It isn't a sense memory, though. Perhaps something in Valerie's voice had told me that she's lying. Or something in her body language. It's not there now.

And whatever the lie is, she has had time to think it through, to hone and perfect it. It will not be easy to find out what her lie is, or why she's telling it.

Rhys says Jimmy's feeling a bit sleepy and doesn't want company, so he's thinking he might pop out for a bit – only he doesn't want to go far because he needs to be able to look in on Jimmy every now and then to make sure he's all right.

Valerie says, "Why not pop into Harry's casino? It's only a step away."

And I have a lightbulb moment. Lianna's passport turned up in that casino, Ferghal haunts it – and Harry Brown owns it. Something is going on in there.

Màiri's Mental Note: The casino is at the centre of a web. Investigate it.

Rhys says that he's not a gambling man and he'll go for a walk.

Now I'm torn. I've had no chance to talk to Rhys yet and I want to, but I need to confront Valerie with her lies. Then Rhys says he'll be back in a few minutes, so I stay with Valerie.

As soon as Rhys has gone, Valerie begins to talk. "Màiri, I'm worried. You know, I told the Sûreté that I left the Tower early to get a bite to eat – and I did. But I came back... and I don't want to tell them that, but if it will help Lianna, then I will tell the Sûreté. But I would hate to do that if it is not necessary. Do you think Lianna needs me to talk to the gendarmes?"

"Why did you come back later?"

"I was on my way out to the food van to get a bite before they closed and then I was going to get the group's tickets and go home. But I met Harry and Ferghal as they were coming in."

"So you stopped for a chat?"

"Yes, and Harry said to come and have supper in the casino. So of course I said I'd love to."

But she gives a tiny shiver. So she's lying about something. What can it be? Obviously, she did want to have supper in Harry Brown's casino... and everything about her body posture except that teeny-weeny quiver says that she's telling the truth.

Teachers have to learn early on how to spot whether a pupil is telling the truth or not. Even naturally truthful students will lie their heads off to protect a friend. So we become experts at reading body language.

Valerie's body language is confusing. At one and the same time, it says that she is lying and that she is not lying...

Màiri's Mental Note 2: Something happened when Harry and Ferghal came

"And you went back to the ticket booth with Harry Brown and Ferghal?"

"With Harry. I needed the group's tickets and he wanted me to translate for him to the office staff – his French isn't very good. Ferghal didn't come with us. He was sorting out some bits and pieces for Harry at the Tower."

Again, that puzzling riff in her body language. Then it comes to me. She isn't lying – she's leaving out something important. What could it be? How can I get her to tell me?

Màiri's Mental Note 3: What is Valerie hiding?

"Oh? What did Harry want you to translate?"

"We didn't get to the head of the queue. Harry said that he needed to check some stuff and we could come back to the booth later."

"Couldn't Ferghal check the other stuff to let you and Harry stay in the queue?"

"No, Ferghal was at the Tower. And you know, Màiri, there were people going up and down in the lift all the time, so I don't understand how anyone could have been killed."

"Yes, it's all very odd. So what was Ferghal doing?"

"Oh, he was taking a lot of measurements for Harry, because they're going to have some kind of celebration there with fireworks. Ferghal was arranging where all the pieces would go."

Màiri's Mental Note 4: Fireworks AFTER Bastille Day? And why Harry Brown's?

That's definitely off. Bastille Day was more than a month ago, July 14th. Why would there be fireworks at the Eiffel Tower near the end of August? And why would the arrangements for a large-scale pyrotechnics display be entrusted to a local casino owner? It's a technical job.

Even if Harry Brown is in charge, why would he choose a technically unqualified hanger-on to handle the set-up? It's bound to be against safety regulations.

I need some time to think about all of this, and to work out what Valerie's not telling me.

"Well, Valerie, it seems as if everyone was being pretty nice to each other. So why didn't you tell the police all this?"

Her eyes drop to her lap and she starts picking at her nails.

"Because I shouldn't have been in the casino. I just had to pick up the tour tickets and then my time was my own, but I'm not allowed to go into places like casinos when I'm managing a tour."

She swallows hard. "If I tell the Sûreté, maybe I'll lose my job."

So Valerie truly has been worried for Lianna, but also she's worried for herself. And not just about her job. Something else is at stake. Something more important to her than her job.

I'll get no more out of her right now, so I change tack.

"What about Aileen?"

Valerie is puzzled. "What about her?"

"How does she know Harry?"

"Does she know him? Harry never said."

"Senga said they were talking on the train."

Valerie shakes her head. "I didn't notice."

"Well, what about Harry's wife? Why did she say that he'd been home all night?"

"She probably thought he was. They live in rooms behind the casino."

"But she must have known he'd gone out. He brought you back for supper."

"Oh, they never eat an evening meal together. Harry likes Northern English cooking, and he doesn't like to have wine with meals. Amélie hates all British food and she's a wine buff, so long ago they decided the only meal they'd eat together would be breakfast."

"Doesn't sound as if supper with him was much fun for you."

She shakes her head. "We ate in the casino. They have a marvellous buffet and lots of wine."

Unless Valerie is lying rather than just hiding something from me – and I don't think she is, not about Harry Brown – then Charlie Stout was murdered between 10 p.m. and 10:30 p.m.

That ought to mean Lianna will go free. She couldn't have murdered him at 10 p.m. and still have been in Hôtel Albert at 10:16 p.m.

But I am not jubilant the way I was on Sunday morning.

Perhaps Inspector Clermont will decide that this is not a new fact. Perhaps he will schedule a magistrate's hearing. And if he does, perhaps the magistrate will decide that Valerie is lying. Or that Charlie Stout could have been murdered and thrown from the Tower earlier that night in spite of the lift full of people constantly going up and down. Or that something else could have happened.

I can't go to Inspector Clermont until I have more evidence.

I need to be certain that the next time I go to Inspector Clermont, he has no choice but to free Lianna. I don't think that I can face another morning like this morning, and I don't think that poor Lianna would be able to stand it either.

And I am still worried about the odd sensation I have that the Major is using me as bait – bait for what? It's a chilling feeling because it makes me realise how little I actually know about Major Ellis Peverel, the not-so-ancient relict...

There's also that tiny thought trying to get my attention, that important elusive little thought. The sense memory. It's there again now, although fainter.

Something about where I am now is in some way similar to where I was when the thought first came to me... and it also has something to do with me sitting in a café eating...

But how could I have been sitting at a table in the lobby of the Hôtel Albert and also sitting in a café when the thought first came to me?

It doesn't make any sense!

What makes complete sense, though, is getting something to eat now. Valerie doesn't want any food – no wonder she's so tiny – but I order a steak sandwich with *pommes frites*.

"Valerie, thank you for coming to me like this. It does make a big difference. It might help to free Lianna. But it might not. So I don't think we should go to the police just yet."

Valerie's entire body sags just a smidgin with release of tension, and I realise how worried she'd been. She's a nice person, and she feels for Lianna. But there is something she's still hiding. Something more than her job will be put at risk if she goes to the police.

I wonder what it could be?

On impulse, I decide to share a small part of my notes with Valerie.

The Major would disapprove, and maybe that's part of why I'm doing it. Maybe I'm feeling a little contrary.

But I don't think so. I'm offering Valerie a key to a hidden doorway, a share in a secret; and I'm pretty sure I'm doing that because I'm hoping to get her to trust me, to relax and open up, so she'll let the truth slip out before she knows what she's said.

Anyway, as I'm digging out my notebook, I'm busy explaining to Valerie the ways I've been working with the Major to get all the facts from the *dossier* files clear, searching for answers.

I'm just beginning to realise how much I relied on Ellis when I still trusted him.

And I'm really sad because I don't trust him anymore.

If I'm being honest, I'm not even being fair to him, because what has he done? Nothing.

But the certainty that I'm being used persists. I know – without knowing how I know – that the Major has his own reasons for being kind to me, and that his reasons have nothing to do with kindness.

M ajor Peverel registers as a temporary member and goes straight into the casino.

Harry Brown is standing close to the Baccarat tables. A heartbeat later, the Major is standing beside him. "Afternoon, Harry. Long time no see."

Harry Brown's memory for faces is excellent. He's pretty certain the only place he's seen this upper-crust type before was at the Hôtel Albert during Clermont's investigation.

"Don't believe I've had the pleasure." he begins, but the Major cuts him off

"Nine years ago, Harry. At the Old Bailey. The French must have pretty liberal gaming regs."

For once, Harry loses his rag. "I might have known that blackmailing little sod had a partner. How much?"

"You've got me wrong, old son. I don't want your filthy lucre. I want to know when you last saw the blackmailing little sod. And don't try to lie to me. Let's go through to your office…"

Why not? Harry thinks. *This chap already knows about the only thing from my past I've got to hide, and maybe I'll learn something from him that helps me with the mess we're in now.*

When they get to Harry's office Major Peverel immediately takes the seat facing the desk, so Harry moves across the room to sit at his desk. Harry doesn't give that a moment's thought, it's the natural thing for him to do.

But in crossing to sit behind his desk Harry momentarily turns his back on the Major, which is what Peverel is watching for. His hand flashes out, and fastens a bug so tiny that it cannot be seen to the underside of Harry's desk.

The Major carelessly crosses his legs, shaking out his trouser legs, which cascades a host of even tinier bugs onto the carpet, just in case the undetectable bug on the underside of the desk gets detected.

"So, which of your many misdeeds did that slimy toad know about, old son?"

"Nothing that could hurt me." Harry grins. "Just an old, old, tax fiddle. And me de-domiciled more'n three years, so what do I care? He can't touch me."

"Then why did you kill him, my dear chap?"

The shock tactic doesn't work. Harry doesn't get bewildered and anxious to prove he didn't do it. He doesn't blurt out, in his eagerness to be cleared, any usable intel such as the Major had hoped to confuse and frighten him into revealing. Harry doesn't turn a hair. "Not me, matey. It was some female tourist, didn't you hear?"

I've finished writing down what Valerie has told me now, so I turn the little notebook Ellis gave me towards her – unaccountably I feel like crying – and show her how the murder time frame looks with all the differences that she told me made to the timings.

I'm hoping that her conscience will kick in again when she sees how many people are under suspicion and that she'll open up to me about what she's hiding.

Murder Time frame based on times recorded in *dossier*

	9 p.m.	9:15 p.m.	9:30 p.m.	9:43 p.m.
Major Peverel	British Embassy	leaves 11 p.m.		
Harry Brown	in casino	Eiffel Tower	Tower	Eiffel Tower
Ferghal Reilly	in casino	Eiffel Tower	Tower	Eiffel Tower
Valerie	at Eiffel Tower	Eiffel Tower	Tower	Eiffel Tower
Aileen & Senga	in their room			
Jimmy Orville	check in ends	in his room?	in his room?	all night?
Rhys Williams	Checks In	check in ends	visits JO?	in bed??
Màiri	hotel queue	Checks In	dining	dining
Lianna	leaves 8:50 p.m.	at casino, asleep powder room: leaves 10:14		
	BUS/car to			
Charlie Stout	Tower	Eiffel Tower	?	?
Yvonne Stout	hotel queue	hotel queue	Checks In	dining

Suspects

			Rhys	Jimmy
Ferghal Reilly	Harry Brown	Aileen	Williams	Orville

As Valerie takes the notebook to look at the chart, the waiter comes back with my sandwich.

The Hôtel Albert's reception staff may be slower than treacle, but you certainly can't fault their food service.

The waiter places in front of me in rapid succession a tiny paper serviette onto which he puts a glass of iced water, then a bottle of vinaigrette, a salt and pepper set, some cutlery wrapped in a paper napkin, a side dish of *frites,* and the plate with my steak sandwich on it, surrounded by fresh salad.

I am lost in admiration. How can he *do* all that so fast without a tray to carry the things on?

The sense memory is shouting at me – I almost have that elusive thought –

Valerie is beginning to speak. And as I hear her voice, memory comes flooding back to me.

I was sitting in an outdoor café with Valerie, admiring the rapid service and eating my ham and cheese sandwich, when she said "Is there any ex-pat in Paris who doesn't have Ferghal's number?" and I had wondered why Valerie thought of herself as an ex-pat.

I hadn't put that down in my notebook. I'd meant to come back to it later, but I forgot. Well, here's my chance now.

Valerie is saying "Why have you put Ferghal and Harry as suspects? They were with me." Her voice is agitated. The tension is beginning to tell on her; I'm holding her by a thread and if I'm not careful, I'll lose her.

Thinking of how I'd handle this in class helps me there. Learning has to be a fairground ride gleefully jumped on; students don't get good marks if you walk them to answers at gunpoint.

Everything in my voice and manner invites Valerie to jump up on the rollercoaster with me.

"Someone must have done it, and everyone is an unlikely suspect. Besides, they weren't with you absolutely all the time."

I start ticking the unlikely names off on my fingers, and oh! how I wish I were drinking the Major's wonderful tea as I tick!

Index finger. "Mrs Stout, as a wife who doesn't seem to be grieving for her late husband overmuch, is a prime suspect. But she couldn't have done it, she was with me throughout the time-of-murder window."

Middle Finger. "Lianna was the choice of the gendarmes. But we know she didn't do it. On this murder time frame you've helped me to create, she couldn't have done it. Impossible.

Ring Finger. "What about me? I never left Hôtel Albert throughout the period of murder time-frame.

"Rhys. I don't know anything about him. There's no reason to suspect him, but equally there's no reason to rule him out.

"Jimmy. Ditto.

"Senga couldn't have done it. We can rule her out – she couldn't see.

But Aileen could have done it. She hated Stout. Senga alibis her, but without her specs, a bolster in the bedclothes would have fooled Senga.

"Yourself. A lot of people saw you all around the Tower, Valerie. You're well known, and you weren't ever alone there for long. (I keep to myself a dawning suspicion that she'd been alone long enough to have killed Tax Charlie if she'd wanted to. Why would she want to?)

"Ferghal. He came to the Tower with...

"Harry Brown, and they were with you most of the time. How did they get there? Did Mr Brown drive?"

Valerie nods.

"And you drove yourself there?"

She nods.

"I meant to ask you before, but I forgot, when we were chatting the other day, you said that it would have been no trouble to take Mr Stout with you, but you didn't say whether you took him or not?"

"No, I didn't take him. He said that he needed to attend to a little errand first. He went into the casino. I drove to the Tower alone."

The casino again. It keeps cropping up. Something is going on in there, I feel sure. What little errand could Tax Charlie have had in Harry Brown's casino?

"So you weren't the last person to see Mr Stout alive after all, Valerie. The last time you saw him he was going into the casino. Other people must have seen him there."

Looking relieved, Valerie nods. "I didn't think of that, but you're right. Mr Stout went into the casino about ten to nine. And I went and got my car and drove to the Tower."

Then she looks anxious again. "I have not said I was the last person to see him alive. I don't know why the police put in the *dossier* that I did. You remember, I said that to you when we were talking in the café."

That wasn't quite what she'd said, but I let it pass. More than ever, I want to know what's going on in that casino.

Me and Ellis had worked out that Tax Charlie couldn't have been killed before 9:30 p.m. because he left the hotel at 8:45 p.m. and so he couldn't have reached the top of the Tower and had the quarrel that resulted in his death before then.

But if he went into the casino first, that changes everything.

Now I need to find out when he left the casino. He might only have been there five minutes, but he could have been there as long as an hour and still have travelled to the Tower in time to get killed during the period when the medical report says it was possible that he died.

And – it suddenly occurs to me – it's most likely that he was killed just after the last tourist party went down in the lift, because no one saw him, not according to what the *dossier* says. Although it has been wrong about other things, and might be wrong about this too.

I decide that I'd better reassure Valerie before I start asking her about her past.

"You were at the Tower during part of the period when the murder could have happened, Valerie, but you were always with someone, isn't that right? A lot of people saw you. Major Peverel and I spoke to some of them."

Valerie stops to think. Then she relaxes. "Yes. I was always with someone or in some place where many people saw me. I was only alone when I was driving there."

"How long was the drive? About twenty minutes?"

"A little less. Traffic was light. I got there about five past nine. So I parked and went straight to the ticket booth, but there was a long queue. It moved slowly. After a few minutes, I went out to the food van to get a filled croissant for my supper."

"And that's when you met Ferghal and Harry Brown coming in?" Valerie nods.

"They came by car too?"

"Yes. Harry has a Daimler."

"But you didn't actually go to the van because Harry Brown invited you to supper."

Valerie nods again. "That's right." But her eyelids flicker and she gives a tiny shiver. There's a lie somewhere in what she's saying, that's certain. I need to know what the lie is.

"And about what time was that, Valerie?"

"I'm not quite sure. Perhaps quarter past nine? No, later – maybe twenty past. Or even twenty-five past. I was right at the back of the queue for a few minutes before I gave up waiting, and so probably it was a little after twenty past, close to twenty-five past."

And she glances away as she says it, she can't meet my eye. So she's lying about the times. Why? What else is she lying about?

"So then you went back into the ticket booth queue with Harry?"

"Yes, the queue had gone down quite a bit, and I was close enough to the booth window to see that Jean-Luc was on duty. He's rather a sweetie. We gave each other a little wave."

"But Harry hurried you away. Why?"

"We'd gone back into the queue because I needed the group's tickets and Harry wanted me to translate for him – but then he said the queue was moving too slowly and he couldn't wait."

"Why not? What was he doing that was urgent?"

Valerie stares at me. "Do you know, I have no idea? He just asked me to help him, so of course I did."

"You're always very helpful, Valerie. Harry Brown is lucky to have you as a friend. How did you come to meet him?"

"Ferghal introduced us, I think. He's very sociable."

"Ah, yes, I remember you were saying the other day how the British ex-pats living in Paris are like a social club, almost. Whereabouts are you from yourself, Valerie?"

"Aveyron. It's very beautiful there, hills and little farms. My aunts still live on a tiny farm nestled in the hills."

"Oh, how lovely! And where do your parents live?"

Valerie's face clouds and for a moment I think that she will burst into tears, but instead her sad look changes to hatred. "My mother died when I was nine. My aunts have always been my family."

"I'm so sorry for your loss. And your father couldn't take care of you when your mother went to her reward?"

"Wouldn't, more like!" she spits out. I can see it's the thought of her father that had brought hatred to her sweet face. "I never met him until recently. He treated my mother very badly."

"I'm sorry to hear that, Valerie. So many men have no sense of responsibility." I say that with feeling, remembering Brian's irresponsible behaviour. But Valerie doesn't respond, so I try again. "Then you were a little girl when you were living in London?"

"How did you know I had lived in London?"

I guessed. She doesn't have a noticeable accent, and there's no lilt or cadence in her voice. If you're from Scotland, you never lose the lilt, or the cadence if you're from Wales. So she's most likely English, and there's less accent in London than in other parts of England.

"I think you mentioned it when we were chatting the other day."

The Major stumps into the lobby just then, and I was never happier to see him, because his arrival distracts Valerie from my questions about her roots.

S cant minutes after his arrival, I'm being ushered me through the revolving doors of Hôtel Albert by the Major en route to his own hotel for tea. I'm not quite sure how he managed to do that without giving offence to Valerie – or how he persuaded me!

But I'm relieved to see Ferghal coming through the other side of the revolving doors with a couple of his pals from the casino. It's good to know that Valerie will have some company.

"H ello, Valerie."
Valerie swims up from her ocean of unhappy thoughts to see Ferghal's battered face smiling down at her, with two of Harry's bouncers standing behind him.

Instantly she remembers an important meeting on the other side of town that she's late for and begins to rise, ready to rush off. But before she can get out more than the first word of her apology, Ferghal leans down, catches her arm and murmurs quietly into her ear.

"Wheesht now, Valerie. You'll not be wanting to disoblige Harry, *not when the two of us were so helpful to you on Friday,* and to be sure your friends that you're rushing off to can wait a bit, can't they? No problemo, then."

Seeing no way out, Valerie tries to smile. "What can I do to help, Ferghal?"

"There's the lass. Go on over to reception, and get the key for Room 101. Tell them Màiri's in with the gendarmes, and asked you to fetch a few of Lianna's things along to her."

"I can't do that, Ferghal. They won't give me a guest's room key."

"To be sure they will, Valerie, and you in charge of the tour, and knowing her room number, and making odd requests on behalf of guests night and day. For certain sure they'll give you the key, Valerie, so run along now and get it."

One of the bouncers pipes up. "Harry said to break the door down."

"Aye, Patrice, if we had to. That's what Harry said, if we had to. Isn't that what the man said, Alec?"

Alec nods.

"But we don't have to, because here's Valerie happy to help us, isn't that right, Valerie?"

Valerie is anything but happy to help them, but she doesn't want Ferghal saying any more about what had happened on Friday night at the Eiffel Tower.

"I'll try to get the key, but you know I'll have to go up to the room alone or they'll think it's very strange."

"No problem, Valerie, we'll just wait for you upstairs."

Valerie watches until they are hidden around the bend in the stairs, and then goes over to the reception desk and rings the bell.

Exactly as Ferghal had predicted, the hotel staff give her Màiri's room key without asking awkward questions; they even ask her if she wants to take Màiri's things out of the hotel safe.

Thankfully disclaiming any desire to do so, Valerie picks up the giant brass key fob engraved 101, and begins climbing the stairs.

The Major
Comes Clean

Chapter 11 The Major Comes Clean

6 p.m. Monday, 17th August, 1970

Hôtel Marquis, Rue Greneta, Paris, France

I'm sitting across from Ellis on one of the sofas in the amazing sitting room at his hotel pretty soon, drinking his marvellous tea and savouring it as always, but finding it hard to talk.

However, I don't need to talk, because Ellis starts the conversational ball rolling.

"Been a difficult day for you, Màiri." His voice is quiet and gentle. "You're bearing up well, old girl."

I fumble out my notebook. Since I'm here, we might as well compare notes.

But Ellis reaches across and takes the notebook from my hand, putting it down on my side of the little table where the tea things sit.

"You're upset with me, Màiri. Upset that Lianna is still with the gendarmes, of course. But also upset with me. What have I done?"

"You haven't done anything." That's true, but he isn't going to believe it, because I *am* upset with him; and although he's almost a stranger to me – we've only known each other three days – he knows me well enough to read my feelings.

"Màiri, did you ever wonder why I'm in Paris?"

I shake my head. I want to say that I've never given a moment's thought to why he's in Paris. That all I'm thinking about is how to free Lianna. But that's simply not true. I've been dying of curiosity about all the question marks hovering around Ellis Peverel's actions ever since he first raged at Charlie Stout on the train.

But I don't want to discuss it now that he's giving me the chance because – I'm incredulous to recognise – I'm *hurt* that he's using me. Why on earth should I feel hurt by anything he does? Come Friday morning when I get on the train to Istanbul – when *Lianna and I* get on that train – I'll never see him again. And then I astonish myself by blurting out, "I know that you're using me as bait. I'm the goat tethered in the clearing for the tiger to eat."

Ellis chokes back a laugh. "Oh, my dear girl! If you knew how hard we've all been working to prevent the tiger from eating you." His face straightens and he reaches across to take my hand and pat it. "This is no laughing matter, is it, old girl? You're upset and you're frightened and now you probably think I'm laughing at you. I promise you, I'm not laughing at you."

He lets go of my hand and leans back in his chair, stroking his moustache. "I'd better come clean, hadn't I? If you know that you're in danger it's less frightening for you if you also know that you're being protected."

In that miraculous way he has – I wonder if there's a noiseless call switch somewhere – he has summoned one of the silently gliding waiters. "Chocolate cake for the lady, please."

He won't explain until I've started to eat the cake. He's right as usual. I feel a little better when I've swallowed a couple of mouthfuls.

"Màiri, I'm sort of a policeman. Part of a joint task force. We're working with Interpol. We've been watching some people whom we think are moving weapons across Europe."

Now I remember him saying, that first day *"...best border team I know."*

"One of them is a Senegalese woman who approached you and your friend on the ferry. We don't know who she's working with. We don't know why she was here. But we do know that she hasn't been in France since early on Saturday, and that she didn't use any of her previous aliases. We think that possibly she left France on your friend's passport."

He can see that I want to know more.

"I can't tell you any more than that."

I go on forking up cake, waiting for him to go on.

"A local police team is keeping an eye out for your safety, Màiri, as I am. And you know that I'm trying to help you to clear your friend of the murder charge laid against her, but frankly, until we've run this crew in, the local lockup is probably the safest place for her."

He leans forward, looking fierce.

"I won't let you be harmed, Màiri."

I finish eating the chocolate cake, and pick up my notebook. It's astonishing how much more cheerful I feel, considering that nothing has changed for the better.

Lianna is still a captive in the French justice system, facing trial for a murder she had nothing to do with, and although I'm not Major Peverel's tethered goat, I'm likely the target of a gang of gun runners, which is worse. But at least I know that Ellis isn't using me; and while there's no reason why that should make me feel better, it does.

"Thank you, Ellis."

Ellis glances at his watch. "I have to go, Màiri, I'm late for a meeting. Won't you stay here and have some more tea? I'll be back in time to give you dinner." He smiles at me, and again I am struck by the charm of his smile. "We can compare notes then, eh?"

One of the silent waiters has glided in. "More chocolate cake."

And Ellis is gone.

<hr />

Valerie finds, when she gets to Room 101, that the door is wide open. Obviously, Patrice and his co-worker Alec weren't willing to wait for a room key – the door lock is broken. Fleetingly she wonders how they knew which room is Màiri's.

Five suitcases and a small travelling case have had their locks bashed in and then ripped open – it's obvious that this luggage can never be used again.

The casino bouncers are tossing clothes, books, and small ornaments all over the room at such speed that Valerie is almost overwhelmed with vertigo. She stands there looking at things being propelled in every direction in a blur of blinding motion. She can't imagine how hurling things about will help them to find whatever they're searching for.

Ferghal stands off to one side, his hands jammed into his pockets, looking sulky.

Quietly, Valerie begins to back away. She can't get involved in this; she'd better go back down to reception. She hopes that before she reaches the desk, she can think of a plausible lie about why she's returning the key so soon.

Ferghal catches sight of her. He slips noiselessly from the room, closing the door over as he leaves, and moves off silently in her wake.

I'm feeling worn out and a little grimy. That was a lovely pot of tea, and the chocolate cake was delicious, but I'm not comfortable. A bath would perk me up. There's plenty of time before dinner for me to go back to the Hôtel Albert to have a bath, and maybe a nap, and change into a nice dress.

Just in case Ellis returns earlier than expected, I scribble a little note for him.

Valerie lets Ferghal handle the return of the room key at the Hôtel Albert reception, which he does without any embarrassment. The clerk doesn't appear to notice how quickly she has returned, or that she doesn't have any of Lianna's things.

"Where have you parked?" Ferghal asks after they pass through the revolving doors, and with horror, Valerie realises that now he wants her to drive him somewhere.

"You are not returning to the casino?"

"With them two upstairs just asking for trouble? Not a bit of it. If I'm anywhere in the picture Harry will put the blame on me for this. No, Valerie, you and me are going to the Tower now to make sure that everything is ship-shape."

"Must we?"

They have reached Valerie's little Peugeot and Ferghal lifts the keys out of her hand.

"I'll drive, Valerie, you look a bit down in the mouth."

It seems that she must. But she tries to get out of it.

"Take the car, Ferghal. You are welcome. But you do not need me – and I have some matters to attend to, work to do..." Valerie trails off because now Ferghal is gripping her wrist.

In a mockery of courtesy, he is opening the passenger door of her car for her and pushing her into the passenger seat.

E llis Peverel has arrived at the offices of the Direction générale de la sécurité extérieure, and is ushered straight into Tristan Toussaint's office.

After brief greetings and briefer amenities, Ellis settles down to put Tristan in the picture – which means making his report backwards, because with the minimum of delay, a listening team must be put onto recording and interpreting the sound stream now being sent from Harry Brown's office.

When the necessary arrangements have been put in train, Tristan puts his feet up on his desk and sips his coffee whilst gazing at Ellis with a fond but irritated eye.

"Ah, my dear chap," he says gently (for using an English idiom is Tristan's favourite method of delivering a mild reproof, an idiosyncrasy well known throughout his bureau). "Two hours of priceless intel lost to us forever, what were you thinking of?"

Ellis isn't in the least put out; he knows Tristan's methods of old and there is nothing this man can do which would surprise him. "Alors, mon ami," he returns, also gently, the spoof finding its mark. Tristan throws up his hand in the gesture of a fencer conceding the hit.

So Ellis grins and continues in his normal manner. "Come off it, old boy. One hour, if that, and you know as well as I do that she's priceless to us. I had to reassure the asset as my top priority, you know that. I got here as quickly as was compatible with the higher need."

"Perhaps, my dear confrère, she is indeed priceless to you, and for you there is no higher priority. But come –" as Ellis sits dumbfounded, trying to work out if Tristan really means what he seems to have said. "The situation is very serious. My colleagues have established that there is a bomb here in the centre of Paris. We must discover where. We must know who is responsible. Think you, could it be this bad hat of yours?"

But Ellis is already shaking his head. "He's small potatoes, at least, he was. Who knows what connections they make in prison? Who knows how much resentment being there breeds? Or how strong the desire for revenge grows?" He pauses and smooths his moustache, thinking.

"But I'll be surprised if Harry has anything to do with a bombing. Weapons smuggling, yes. There's a ton of money in it. And I'd love to know how he laid his hands on that casino. His terrorist friends may have arranged that for him. It may be their front. But there's no money in a bombing, just a lot of danger for him... Why would he get involved?"

Tristan shrugs. "The listening team will be set up now, let us go through there and find out what we can. More coffee?" Without waiting for an answer, Tristan orders coffee sent to the listening post, and the two friends walk down the corridor to discover the state of play.

Valerie hasn't completely abandoned hope that Ferghal will let her go once they reach the Tower, but she knows that isn't likely to happen. It's cruel of him, but Ferghal is an odd man. All charm on the outside, cold as ice inside. If he happened to think of doing it, he'd boil her bones for soup and be puzzled if anyone told him that he shouldn't have.

How she wishes she had never met him. But it's too late now.

"Ferghal, why are you taking me to the Tower?"

"Need a lookout, don't I?" He looks and sounds sulky, as if it's her fault that whatever he needs a lookout for wasn't done earlier. "Why did you have to push that taxman over the edge? We had to leave the job at the Tower half-done."

Valerie doesn't ask: *"What job?"* Ferghal is annoyed, and that's never good.

"Ferghal, you know I didn't push him off the Tower. He was too heavy for me to push off. Why do you say I pushed him off? You and Henri threw him off. It is not my fault."

"It is your fault. You pushed him into Harry and Harry dropped... Never mind what. After he saw that, Harry had to get rid of him. There wasn't time to finish the job. It's all your fault. And don't think you can blame me and Henri. We've got that recording, remember? Who do you think will believe you if you say it was us?"

Valerie shudders. No one will believe her, no matter what she says. If Harry plays anyone that recording, everything she has been hiding all these years will be out in the open. She will be despised.

"You should never have come here. You will not go away again. You horrible, wicked, cruel man, you deserve to burn in hell forever." When they hear her saying that, they will arrest her, the guillotine will follow

swiftly. And it would be a relief, to die swiftly, compared to living with her shame once the truth is known.

I'm strolling down Rue du Faubourg Saint-Denis, idly glancing into shop windows as I pass them. One very smart dress shop has a model in the window that reminds me of Valerie.

Next door is a bar, where Bread's "Make It With You" plays loudly. Perhaps it has been put on the jukebox by the tipsy Englishman who is standing in the doorway inviting me in.

Quickly moving on towards the Hôtel Albert, I suddenly flash back to Valerie sitting in their bar with her face turned away, muttering *"My father comes to Paris after all these years and **he** (the words fade) silly fireworks"* and all at once I **know**.

Tax Charlie is the heartless father who abandoned Valerie and her mother.

The casino bouncers have reduced Room 101 to an absolute shambles. Some small things are crushed underfoot, no telling what they once might have been, and Patrice is standing in the centre of the room, trampling down Màiri's clothes and looking a little lost.

"It is not here, Alec."

"It must be here. Look under the mattress, right?"

Before Alec has quite finished speaking, Patrice has produced a sharp-edged knife. Tearing off the bedclothes on the nearer of the two beds, he attacks the mattress with his knife.

I see that drunken Englishman has left the bar now and is following me down the street. I quicken my steps. Is *nowhere* in Paris safe for an unaccompanied woman?

Alec surveys the absolute devastation of Room 101, where the over-enthusiastic Patrice has savaged the mattresses and pulled down the curtains. He wonders where the detonator could possibly be. The washroom? In hotels like this the washrooms are shared, but there's no other place left to look.

Alec glances around, in case some hidey-hole has escaped his notice.

Hey, where's Ferghal?

In my haste to escape the tiresome Englishman, I haven't been watching where I was going. Abruptly, I bump into someone. It turns out to be a good-looking young Frenchman who takes the chance contact as an invitation to introduce himself.

Now I'm trying to escape from two importunate Lotharios at the same time. What *is* it about the Paris streets once evening sets in?

I quicken my steps – again – and with relief reach the *pension*, pushing through its revolving door partition as fast as I can.

Alec closes over the busted door of Room 101, so that the ransacking of Màiri's room will not be instantly obvious to every chance passer-by, and jerks his head at the door of the adjoining washroom.

Patrice needs no more elaborate invitation. He charges into the washroom. Seconds later he spots Lianna's glossy striped sponge bag.

With a triumphant cry, Patrice tosses it out to Alec. Alec catches and unzips the bag. No detonator. He shakes his head at Patrice.

***

I walk up to reception and find that a clerk is already standing at the desk, so for once the service is less snail-like.

"Ah, Miss Maguire, we do not expect you so soon." says the clerk after he hands me my giant brass key fob. "Your friend tell us you visit the Sûreté."

I've turned towards the stairs with a murmured "Merci", but at this unexpected news, I swing back. "My friend?"

"The little *mademoiselle*. So pretty. She help *pensionnaires* English."

"Do you mean our tour guide, Valerie?"

The clerk nods and smiles.

I'm puzzled. "When did Valerie say that?"

The clerk spreads his hands. "Some minutes."

Why should Valerie think that when I left with Ellis we were going to the Sûreté? Ellis hadn't said that. Not that it's important. Murmuring "Merci" again, I head upstairs for my bath.

***

Patrice has emptied Màiri's laundry bag into the shower tray. No detonator. The last possible hiding place has been ransacked without success. They're out of options.

"It is not here, Alec. We need to tell Harry."

"You heard what he said, right? *Don't come back without it.* We need to find this woman and make her tell us what she's done with it."

A woman's head rises into view as she climbs the last few stairs, and Alec reaches around the half-open washroom door to nudge Patrice. But Patrice needs no nudge. He has seen Màiri and is already reaching for his knife.

I've reached the top step when I see one of Ferghal's friends standing next to my room. But where's Ferghal? And why is his friend at my room door? If he wants to see me, why isn't he waiting downstairs? And where's *his* friend?

I'm about to step forward and ask what's going on when some formless instinct warns me that I shouldn't, a split second before the washroom door slams open and a hurtling figure charges toward me.

The instant that rhinoceros charge begins, I'm racing back down the stairs. Screaming for help. Stumbling in high heels never meant for running in. Tumbling down the curving staircase with that menacing figure racing after me.

Is he gaining on me? I twist around as I half-run, half-fall, down the stairs – just as his arm rises to throw – but that violent movement is frustrated by the other man. He's snarling "Don't! We need her alive! Drop it!"

I gasp when I hear "alive". They aren't going to kill me. I don't know what other harm they might do me in the middle of a public place – but I don't want to find out.

I round the bend in the stairs, coming into view of the lobby – there isn't a soul in sight. My screams for help have not roused the snails at reception.

I try desperately to remember the French for "Help me"

"M'aidez!" I scream "M'aidez!" as I tear down the rest of the stairs.

The rhinoceros comes around the bend in the stairs as I gain the lobby. It's still empty.

So I'm racing for the doors, screaming "M'aidez!" I'm frightened of going into those doors! They revolve, the madman behind me might manage to pull them back and pluck me out of them. But what better choice do I have?

As I race for the doors, the heel on my right shoe catches in the carpet. At the speed I'm moving there's no chance to ease the pressure. The heel twists, bends, snaps!

My momentum is propelling me forward – there's zero chance I can recover my balance or stop to free the heel. I'm going to fall and the rhinoceros is going to catch me!

There's still no one in sight – the cavalry is not coming.

Instinctively I rise up on tiptoe inside my shoes and race on, going *with* the momentum.

It works! The shoe comes free!

Running on tip-toe as I am now, only my toes are in contact with my shoes. My high heels no longer get in my way – because they aren't touching the ground as I run. Only my shoe-tips are in contact with the ground.

I'm moving faster than ever. I'm at the doors – here goes nothing – I race into the first door partition and push as hard as I can. I'm going to make it!

The revolving door is coming into the street, it's halfway open – it's almost wide enough for me to get out into the street – but not quite.

I can't squeeze myself that thin!

I push harder, but it's no use, the door sticks. A second later a slow drag backwards starts...

Just as I feared, the rhinoceros has caught up and is pulling the revolving partition back into the hotel.

I push desperately. Screaming "M'aidez!" Sobbing with fright. Throwing my whole body forward against the glass partition in a futile attempt to widen the gap far enough for me to skin through it. Miraculously, it *does* move just a fraction!

And suddenly something is holding the door open the wee bit further I need!

I draw in my breath – make myself as thin as I can – stumble out into the street, where strong arms catch me and instantly put me aside.

A blurring figure strides into the door partition I have just escaped from. He pushes on into the hotel. I faint.

When I come to, Ellis is bending over me. "Buck up, old girl. I told you I wouldn't let you be harmed."

Gendarmes are leading away the handcuffed rhinoceros.

"What about his friend?"

Ellis frowns. "Someone was with him?"

"Yes, one of Ferghal's friends from the casino."

He straightens, stroking his moustache.

"And Ferghal?

"No. At least, I didn't see him."

"Hmmm." His hand reaches down and he pulls me to my feet. "Let's get you some tea. And aspirin. And then you can tell me all about it."

Although his hotel is only a few minutes walk away, the Major whistles to summon a taxi. When it pulls up beside us, he unceremoniously bundles me into it.

I understand why he called the taxi when he doesn't get in with me. "Get them to give you some tea and aspirin, and wait for me. I need to look into this."

He says something in rapid French to the driver, who pulls out into the traffic stream, and I see Ellis going back into the Hôtel Albert just as my taxi abruptly rounds the corner.

That's when I realise I'm still clutching my room key.

Chapter 12 Harry's Team in Action

7:11 p.m. Monday, 17th August, 1970

Lucky 8 Casino, Rue du Faubourg Saint-Denis, Paris, France

Harry is searching for a leadership mantra to keep him on point. He draws deep on a Benson & Hedges; the smoke is soothing.

Ferghal has vanished. Patrice is banged up. He won't talk, though. No worries on that front.

Alec has reported utter failure to lay his hands on the detonator.

The little school teacher is temporarily beyond reach, and must be brought back into reach and under Harry's control. Induced to yield up the detonator. And then disposed of.

What would Sun Tzu have to say about all this? Harry can only bring to mind *"The enemy of my enemy is my friend."* Not immediately helpful...

Let's see... Alec has failed to get the detonator so far, but he's a good lad. He's bungled, and that will put him on his mettle. Who to send with him? There's the rub. Who's on the strength that's reliable, and won't talk if he's caught, has got the muscle to grab this tiresome girl, and isn't going to have an attack of conscience when she gets hurt? Maybe Alec will know...

Summoned, Alec's response knocks Harry back.

"There's no lad like that here, not anymore." He muses for a moment, then adds, "And if you want my opinion, boss, it was a mistake to beat Ferghal up, right? He's stupid, right enough. But he's mad for what he calls 'Free Ireland.' He didn't hide that detonator." Alec shakes his head. "He wants to see Paris blown up, right? If he's got it now – but I bet he hasn't – then he's on the job this minute, checking all the wiring connections before he wires it in."

"You're saying, what? You want to go to the Tower and look for him?"

"Nah, he's stupid. And soft-hearted about women. Nah, I'm sayin' this isn't a job for one of the lads, right? It's a job for Gillian. Or easier, that woman who came here..."

"Not Aileen. She'd never go along with it. Just because she wants some tax records altered doesn't make her willing to blow people up. Likely she'd turn us in. Go get Gillian."

Harry lights another smoke. Amélie doesn't like him smoking in the casino; she doesn't like him to enjoy himself much at all, a right killjoy. But what she doesn't know can't hurt him.

Odd notion Alec has there, bringing one of the croupiers into this, and a woman at that. But Gillian will do whatever she's told, and she hasn't a sympathetic bone in her body. Not a bad choice, really....

Alec's idea turns out to be simple enough. Gillian will get the school teacher talking – ask her for the time, or directions, or something, since she doesn't know Gillian (now Harry sees why Aileen had been Alec's preference – the little school teacher would talk to her all day).

And while her attention's on Gillian, Alec will knock her out from behind. Then they'll bundle her into the Daimler and bring her here.

"Sound plan. Go get her." Harry discovers that he's out of smokes. "Gillian! On your way out, get the bartender to send in a packet of Benson & Hedges."

Tristan Toussaint's listening team at Direction générale de la sécurité extérieure have heard and recorded the entire conversation Harry has just had with Alec and Gillian, thanks to the bug Major Peverel had installed when he blagged his way into Harry's office. They flag it at once.

What have they flagged? The bomb threat.

An ops team is instantly despatched to the Eiffel Tower.

What of Màiri's predicament? The listening team don't have sufficient info to act.

Who is the school teacher the bombers are going to kidnap? Where is she located?

The listeners can't send an intervention team to an unknown location to help an unknown target who is about to be accosted by a woman for whom they have no description.

Best they can do is continue to keep a watch on the casino (which has been watched around the clock ever since Ellis had confided in Tristan at the British Embassy) and try to spot the victim when she is being smuggled in – a forlorn hope.

Màiri is on her own... the cavalry isn't coming.

Of course, things would have turned out differently if Tristan had heard that conversation. But he was closeted in an interrogation room with the assailant – who had so far refused to give his name – and the message brought to him simply said that a team had been sent to the Eiffel Tower to check on the possibility that the bomb might have been hidden there.

Things would have turned out differently if Ellis had heard that conversation. But he was on his way to the casino to discover who the second assailant had been, since nothing in the way of useful information had emerged at the Hôtel Albert.

No rescuers are on the horizon.

I'm feeling pretty sick and shaken when the taxi deposits me at the Major's hotel. Before I can open my bag to pay him, almost before I take my hand off the taxi's door handle, he tears off again. I'm not even going to try to work that one out.

As I limp into the foyer, one of the gliding waiters appears and ushers me into the beautiful sitting room. Moments later, a second waiter arrives with a blanket. A third comes in carrying the tea things. The first waiter kneels and removes my broken shoe, and then the other shoe. A fourth waiter arrives with a pair of fluffy slippers. How *do* they do it?

Answering the silent invitation of the blanket, I swing my legs onto the sofa and am at once enveloped in the softest lambswool. I've fallen asleep before they have time to make the tea or bring any aspirin.

When I wake up, it's to find Ellis bending over me again, smiling his delightful smile.

"Feeling better now, are we, old girl?"

I sit up hastily, embarrassed to have been found in disarray.

"Yes, thanks. But I can't sit here, I need to make myself presentable. Oh, just look at me, lying here in fluffy slippers. My heel broke when I was running away from that lunatic."

I remember that once I had thought of Ellis as a lunatic, and blush. This is so embarrassing. I need to stop squirming and go get some shoes. But Ellis is sitting down, so clearly he doesn't think that I'm about to dash off in search of footwear.

"Màiri, I don't think you have much left in the way of shoes. Or clothes. The intruders wrecked your room."

I stare at him, not really taking it in. Where am I going to get some shoes? "I need to get some shoes. What time is it? Are the shoe shops still open?"

He waves his hand, a bit impatiently, I think. "Oh yes, Galerie des Tuileries, Galerie des Arcades, Galeries Lafayette, they're all open until at least ten o'clock tonight. This is Paris, old girl. Everyone shops their heads off."

It was definitely testy, the way he said that. The Major is annoyed for some reason. But I've no time to wonder about why he's annoyed, I need to get some shoes. I struggle to my feet.

Instantly, the Major is by my side, holding my elbow, steadying me. It's really astonishing, the way he can move so fast without seeming to move at all. He shifts his grip to my shoulders, and gently pushes me back down.

"Màiri, you're in shock. You're not going anywhere for a bit. Drink some tea, and in a little while, my doctor will come to see you. I'll go and ring him right now."

And he's gone. Good. I can go get some shoes.

It's easier getting to my feet this time, and I drift out to the lobby and through the lobby to the entrance. I ask the doorman to get me a taxi. Seconds later, he's holding a taxi door open for me. I say that I want to go to Galerie des Arcades.

As I open my bag to tip him, I see my stupid hotel key lying on top of my hairbrush. Oh, yes, I'd still had it in my hand when the Major bundled me into a taxi outside the Hôtel Albert. Well, no time to worry about that. I need to get some shoes. So I tip the doorman and my taxi eases into the traffic stream.

As the taxi pulls into the traffic, Alec and Gillian come around the street corner just in time to spot Màiri sitting in the back of a taxi. It hadn't been easy tracking her to the Hôtel Marquis, and now she's gone.

Alec snarls. Gillian puts her hand out, halting him. "Wait here. I'll talk to the doorman." Smiling her best professional croupier's smile, Gillian speaks briefly to the doorman.

He signals for another taxi. Gillian waves Alec over, tips the doorman, and they are on their way to Galerie des Arcades. As soon as the taxi is out of sight of the doorman, it stops and drops off Alec, who needs to go and get the Daimler.

I'm at Galerie des Arcades almost at once. It's just off the Champs-Élysées. It's beautiful. A tremendously elegant frontage leading into a long glass-covered passageway of gorgeous shops full of the most exotic things, each lovelier than the last.

Where am I going to find, in this exquisite shopping place, anything as simple and utilitarian as a pair of walking shoes? After that terrifying run down the stairs at the Hôtel Albert, I'm in no mood to buy high heels. Some good stout brogues will do me nicely. If I can find them.

I feel terribly self-conscious wandering through this fairyland in fluffy slippers. But I can't see any shoe shops, so what can I do?

I walk a little further in, still not seeing any shoe shops, and a fresh worry assails me. This looks like an extremely expensive place. Do I have enough money on me to buy shoes?

Do I even have my passport with me? I still haven't had time to change any of my Travellers Cheques for francs – I feel like I've been running on a hamster wheel ever since I arrived in Paris, moving faster and faster and never getting anywhere.

And whether that's true or not, I certainly haven't had time to get into another bank to change my Travellers Cheques for francs. Snobby shops like these will accept Travellers Cheques, of course, but not if I don't have my passport.

I'm beginning to scrabble frantically through my bag to see if my passport's in there, when a woman's hand touches me lightly on the arm. "Excuse me, miss, could you direct me to the Ladies Room, please?"

A sixth sense warns me.

Thinking about it later, I realise that it was the slightly accented French voice speaking to me in English that had alerted me to my danger. Why should a random passer-by speak to me in English, if she wasn't English herself? If she knew me for a foreigner, a stranger, why should she ask me for directions to the powder room, when it isn't very likely that a tourist would know where it is, and on all sides there are native Parisiennes who could tell her...

But at the time I didn't think about it at all. I reacted instinctively.

All by itself, my hand closes on my room key and I whirl around just as fast as I can in fluffy slippers – not all that fast but fast enough – and see the man who was with the rhinoceros when he attacked me.

So I reach up as high as I can and hit him alongside the head with the giant brass key fob just as hard as I can.

It's not hard enough.

He staggers, but he comes back fast and mean, a cosh in his hand.

I move instantly, so the cosh only catches me a glancing blow, but my head and face explode with the pain of it.

With every movement I make, my fluffy slippers are sliding on the beautifully smooth paving of this exquisite arcade. I know that if I try to run, I'll slip and fall.

I can't run away.

I can't hit him hard enough to knock him out.

I can't move fast enough to dodge his next blow.

No one is coming to my rescue.

There seems to be no way I can escape from this monster.

But I'm from Glasgow. We ken street fighting there.

True to my heritage, faster than thought, I turn the key sideways, point on, and jab it straight into his eye.

He screams and drops the cosh, bringing his hands up to his eye.

A security guard runs up, far too late to be of any use to anyone. People are shouting. Some are running away.

And I still don't have any shoes.

I wait stoically. Eventually, the gendarmes turn up, and instead of taking me to the pokey they bring me back to the Hôtel Marquise.

That's a surprise, but then I see Ellis standing there in the lobby. I might have known it. He wasn't even there, but somehow he took charge anyway. Well, I should be grateful. It's not as if I *wanted* to go to the pokey.

He takes me into the beautiful sitting room and they bring me tea and aspirin.

The doctor comes and puts a bandage on the side of my head.

Then they all go away, except Ellis, who begins to tell me just how foolish I've been and how lucky I am to still be alive.

At last, he finishes up his gentle lecture on the need to take better care of myself and sits back, smiling his delightful smile and looking rather relieved.

I drink my tea, wondering why I'm resentful of the lecture.

He's right. He's always right.

I should have sat there patiently and waited for his doctor to come and treat me for shock.

If I'd done what Ellis said to do, I'd have saved myself a frightening and painful episode – and when all is said and done, me racing off like that didn't make anything any better.

Yes, the gendarmes have locked up my second set of assailants. So what?

We don't know why those goons trashed my hotel room. We don't know why they attacked me in the middle of the parade of beautiful shops in Galerie des Arcades.

My head hurts. And I don't have any shoes.

But a tiny rebellious part of my mind says "I was OK. No one was there to save me, but I saved myself. What right does the Major have to lecture me anyway, he's not my father."

There's no point in thinking like that, however, and no point in strolling down memory lane. Ellis is right. It's dangerous out there. I blink back to the present.

Lianna is still locked up, and I am no closer to finding evidence that will help to free her.

Of course I'm glad that the Major has discovered more clues that are important to his gun running case, even if a tiny bit resentful about the way he's been using me.

Well, in fairness, he's not really been using me. If I'd done what he wanted me to do, I'd not have been in harm's way. We've been working together because for different reasons we want the same things – some of the time – that's all.

And I still don't understand why that bothers me; why I wish that Ellis wanted to help me not because watching over me might help him to catch his gun runners, but just because he wants to help me. It's a crazy way to feel. What does it matter why he's helping me? Why should I care why he does anything? But I do.

I'm not going to think about it anymore. It's a mystery, and there are more important things to worry about, with weapons turning up all over Europe.

I was amazed when Ellis told me that Paris, which seems so glamourous to us, had its own Troubles and its own IRA – called Organisation Armée Secrète (OAS).

Eerily the same really – the French were oppressing Algeria just like the English oppressing Ireland, and some people were fighting it. But the IRA is fighting to free Ireland. The OAS was fighting to keep Algeria under French rule.

The OAS got disbanded years ago, and Harry Brown has been gathering up people who were unhappy about that to be his own wee army helping him to move weapons.

Harry had been storing them in the Eiffel Tower, pretending that it was stuff for the Bastille Day celebrations, and after that, stuff being stock-piled for the coming New Year celebration.

It's not that I mind helping the Major to catch his gun runners. I *want* to help him catch them. The thought of armed goons running around Paris attacking people is frightening – especially since I'm one of the people being attacked! I just wish... but I'm not going to think about that anymore. I need to talk to Ellis sensibly about what's been happening.

"Ellis, I don't understand. You say that police are watching the Hôtel Albert front and back, and ready to watch my new room too. The gendarmes won't let anyone into the lobby who isn't a guest. And so I'll be safe enough, you say.

"But why did those men attack me in the first place? You said that it had something to do with a woman who approached Lianna and me on the boat? No one did. Our boat journey was uneventful. Do you mean when we met Valerie on the train?"

"Valerie is under suspicion."

My heart sinks. I really like Valerie and I've been hoping that she's got nothing to do with any of this, that she's just as helpless in the face of a cruel fate as Lianna and me.

I want to believe that she's been thrown into this crazy mess for no sane reason, just like us, and is trying to help catch the baddies, like me. But I remember all sorts of worrying things. Maybe she is a part of this plot. Maybe she's in it up to her neck.

"But no, I don't mean Valerie. Someone else approached you, she's our target."

"I don't know who you mean?"

"A Senegalese woman. Tall. Distinctive looking. Does nothing come to mind?"

"No one asked us to do anything, Ellis. We got on the train from Glasgow to London, then went straight to our B&B. We ate our evening meal there, went out to the theatre, came straight back, and went to bed. Next day we got on the boat train first thing in the morning.

"We got on the ferry. We ate lunch at Le Havre and got on the train to Paris, and that's it. Nothing else happened. We spoke to Valerie and Ferghal and Aileen and Senga and the people who served us food and took our tickets, and you. No one else."

But the little voice at the back of my head is screaming again, telling me that we did speak to someone else. Who could it have been?

I think back. Lianna wouldn't go into the refreshment saloon because she thought that she'd seen Charlie Stout. So we stayed on deck. No one else was on deck.

We didn't speak to anyone because there was no one on deck to speak to, until people began pouring out of the refreshment saloon, getting ready to disembark at Le Havre.

"Wait a moment," I say slowly. "There was a woman who spoke to us on the ferry, but it was nothing. She just said that the weather was nice and then she drifted off."

"What did she look like?"

"She was a tall, dark woman and she was in a kind of windbreaker. She had an unusual accent."

"That's our target. What did she say to you, Màiri?
Try to remember every word."

"I think that she said she lives in Le Havre. Yes. I asked her if she would be travelling with us to Paris and she said that she wouldn't be, because she lives in Le Havre. And she said it was a beautiful day with the breeze just right. But it was nothing. She said the weather was nice and admired Lianna's luggage."

Ellis pounces.

"You didn't say anything about her admiring your luggage."

"The woman didn't say anything about luggage, she just looked at Lianna's cases admiringly. People are always admiring Lianna's things. She has beautiful luggage. She HAD beautiful luggage."

I begin to cry.

Then I straighten up again and try to stop. Crying won't help.

"Lianna buys beautiful things, everyone admires them! That woman just looked at the luggage in an admiring way, because Lianna…" I break down again "… her beautiful luggage all cut up, and her lovely sponge bag, it was brand new…"

Wait a minute. There *was* something. I'm quivering.

"Ellis, when I was getting ready for Mass on Sunday, I found a beautiful sponge bag in my luggage. It wasn't mine and it wasn't Lianna's. I wondered how it got into my suitcase..."

"Lost!" Ellis groans. "There was something in that sponge bag and the bo– the people I'm searching for found it."

"No, they didn't. When I found the bag, and I couldn't make the hotel staff understand about Lost Property, I asked the reception clerk to put it into the hotel safe."

Ellis jumps to his feet. "Must make a phone call. You won't run away this time, will you, Màiri?" He smiles that wonderful smile again and I feel so safe, which is crazy, with armed gun runners after me.

"No." I smile mistily back up at him. "I'll wait right here for you, Ellis."

The Major's
Team
in Action

Chapter 13 The Major's Team in Action

9:40 p.m. Monday, 17th August, 1970

Hôtel Marquis, Rue Greneta, Paris, France

Ellis goes straight to his suite and puts in a call to Tristan. This is the big break they have been waiting for. Probably there is something vital to the bombers' plans in that sponge bag. Tristan is swiftly put in possession of the facts.

Tristan moves fast. His people are in the Hôtel Albert within minutes, taking the sponge bag out of the safe, extracting its contents, refilling it with paper and putting it back in the safe.

All of that is done out of sight of any hotel employees, for it is Tristan's plan to use the dummy sponge bag as a lure to draw out the bombers.

Tristan's team bring what they found back to Tristan in his office at Direction générale de la sécurité extérieure. Once the tech team has examined it and they know that the item they've found is a bomb detonator, everyone relaxes. The bombers can't set off their bomb without a detonator.

Of course, they could send for another detonator. But that isn't likely to happen now because Tristan's plan is to let the plotters know right away that Màiri put a sponge bag into the hotel safe, and then to round them up when they go to fetch it.

How to let the bombers know is a tricky question, but a way will be found...

Very soon, a way is found. They have caught the littlest fish at the border, the Eiffel Tower lift attendant, Henri le Blanc. Some regulations infringement of no importance.

But Tristan's department is a well-oiled machine. Years ago, orders had gone out to the border police to detain anyone on the long list of suspected AOS die-hards, and to bring the suspects to Paris for questioning.

Henri le Blanc has been delivered to Tristan's office just when he is most useful. Told that he need not be prosecuted if he co-operates, the man becomes putty in Tristan's hands.

At the Hôtel Marquise, Ellis is arguing with Màiri. He knows that the Hôtel Albert is not a safe place for her, because soon it's going to be full of bombers. But he can't tell her that – the walls have ears.

He is beginning to be exasperated, because she just won't listen to reason.

"Màiri, you have to stay here tonight. We can't fully secure your *pension*. I need you to be here, where I can protect you."

Màiri sniffs. "It was safe enough before you went off to make that phone call."

She tosses her head, those auburn curls flowing distractingly.

What a truly tiresome female she is! Calling attention to the one thing he needs to play down, that his phone call to Tristan has altered the whole playing field and brought the Hôtel Albert into target status.

"I need you to be here, Màiri, where I can protect you."

But the pills the doctor gave her have worked too well, she isn't frightened anymore. Or rather, she's frightened enough to be stubborn and belligerent, but not frightened enough to be eager for protection.

"I will not stay here. It isn't respectable."

The ground of her resistance has shifted. Excellent. "Where would be respectable, Màiri?"

A waiter glides in, beaming, bringing Màiri her mended high heels. They are as good as new, the repairs invisible. She cradles them to her cheek and bursts into tears.

Women!

H arry is exasperated. How hard could it have been, gathering in an unsuspecting woman from a shopping arcade? And those idiots had not only failed, they'd let themselves be caught.

Alec won't talk, of course. But Gillian might. She hasn't got a loyal bone in her body. Harry's not quite sure whether she recognises how foolish it would be to cross him.

He prowls his office, chain-smoking, and the intercom crackles to life. "Harry, someone from the Eiffel Tower to see you. Says it's urgent."

Harry depresses the button. "Send him in." Who could be coming to him from the Tower?

To his surprise, it's that little ferret of a lift attendant. "Thought you'd run for the border?"

"I did, Harry. But that was before..."

When he's heard what Henri has to say, Harry is smiling for the first time since his breakfast in Le Havre. The detonator is almost in his hands. And about time too!

H arry finds that everything after that is smooth sailing. He no longer trusts any of his team, so he drives out to the Tower on his own, and makes sure that everything is in apple pie order.

He sits smoking a celebratory cigarette beside the bomb, looking out over Paris and dreaming of the tropical island that will be his future home. A whole island as his personal possession, his own little kingdom. Not bad for a lad that was raised on free school dinners.

It will be a positive pleasure to blow up Amélie, Harry thinks as he stubs out his cigarette and turns toward the Tower lift, ready to make his way back to the casino. The set-up is perfecto, just waiting for the detonator to be wired in.

When it has been, Harry will take the remote as far away from the blast area as he can, and set off the bomb from inside the private plane that will fly him away from all the devastation. *Tropical maidens, here I come,* he smirks.

H arry decides, as he's going down in the lift, that he can afford to be magnanimous. Ferghal has done a good job of the wiring at the Tower, so he will forgive the Irish lunk the stupidity which almost lost them the detonator. He will allow Ferghal to wire the bomb up.

But can he safely entrust Ferghal with the job of retrieving the sponge bag from the safe? He's screwed up more than once. But on the other hand, he didn't get caught, which is more than Harry can say for his other enforcers.

And then Harry thinks of the perfect person to retrieve the sponge bag. Valerie.

H arry sends for Valerie fifteen minutes later, as soon as he gets back to the casino. She comes to his office pretty quickly, looking suitably beaten down and woebegone. But just to be on the safe side, Harry gives her a little reminder of how thoroughly in his power she is.

"Ah, Valerie, sit down. I've a little job for you. If you do it well, perhaps I'll let you have this." He picks up the mini-recorder and hits playback. Her recorded voice fills the room.

I hate you! click *You should never have come here. You will not go away again. You horrible, wicked, cruel man, you deserve to burn in hell forever.*

"You'd like to have the evidence that you killed poor Mr Stout disposed of, wouldn't you, Valerie?"

But she doesn't rise to the bait. Just sits staring down at her hands. No fun to be had there. He'll have plenty of fun later, though, so no real need to twist the knife any deeper now.

"It's a very easy little job, Valerie. All you have to do is pop along to the Hôtel Albert and tell them the school teacher wants you to get something out of the safe for her."

She shudders, remembering that just before Ferghal had dragged her off to the Tower to be his lookout, the reception clerk had offered to fetch for her whatever it was that Màiri had put into the safe.

She can't imagine why those silly fireworks are so important to Ferghal and Harry, anyway, or why he needed a lookout. But it is safest not to ask, with those two. If she asks the wrong question, Harry might decide to strangle her.

Harry sees her shudder and nods to himself, satisfied. Some history there. He doesn't need to know what it is, but she'll be able to lay her hot little hands on the bag.

"You're fetching a pretty toiletries bag, Valerie. Bring it here to me. Don't open it. Clear?"

"Yes, Harry. I'll go now."

The listening team flags that conversation and sends it straight through to Tristan's office. Tristan frowns over it. A decision has to be made. Does he want to pick up Valerie on her own? On the whole, he thinks not. He has a subordinate place a call to the Hôtel Albert and tell his people to let her pick up the bag. Then he decides to run this development by Ellis, who may have something to contribute.

The staff at Hôtel Marquise interrupt the ongoing dispute between Ellis and Màiri to bring him a note. He asks Màiri to wait a few minutes and leaves in order to confer with Tristan on the telephone.

Once Tristan has put him in the picture, Ellis thinks that this is a good opportunity to kill two birds with one stone. He tells Tristan what he has in mind, and Tristan sees no reason to refuse his old friend. Not that he thinks the idea will work, but what is there to lose?

E llis goes back to Màiri as soon as he puts down the phone, to tell her about the bombers, information which up until now he has kept to himself.

He explains why he's opening up about that now. It's because he wants Valerie to confess and he thinks that Màiri has a better chance of getting her to confess than anyone else does.

I cannot believe my ears.

The Major is showing himself in his true colours now, an oppressor like all the English!

He says that Valerie killed Charlie Stout. He plays back for me, on a little recorder, the proof of her guilt.

I hate you! click *You should never have come here. You will not go away again. You horrible, wicked, cruel man, you deserve to burn in hell forever.*

I've thought before now that maybe Valerie is the killer. Although when I think how sweet she is, it's hard to believe. But even if she killed Stout, she has the right to a fair trial.

It's wrong for the poliss to trap her into a confession. And to be asking *me* to abuse her trust!

But then he tells me about the bomb planted at the Eiffel Tower.

And finally, he delivers the clincher. "Màiri, it's Monday night. You've only three days left to prove your friend innocent. Do you want her to suffer the penalty that Valerie should? Get Valerie's confession, and your friend will go free."

Valerie leaves the Hôtel Albert, tightly clutching the toiletries bag, and she is at once picked up by Tristan's team and brought to the Hôtel Marquise, where Ellis waits in the lobby. He tells her that Harry is planning to bomb Paris, and had sent her to pick up the detonator for the bomb.

Màiri Searches for The Truth

Chapter 14 Màiri Searches For The Truth

10:30 p.m. Monday, 17th August, 1970

Hôtel Marquis, Rue Greneta, Paris, France

I find that it has come to this, when all is said and done. There is no doubt that Valerie killed Charlie Stout. Considering how he treated her and her mother, I can't help feeling that he deserved it. I'm sorry that Valerie must stand trial for his murder – as she said herself: *It's a pity that he ever came to Paris.*

It seems cruelly unfair to take advantage of her trusting nature.

But it's her or Lianna – who is absolutely blameless – and so I harden my heart and set about extracting a confession from Valerie.

"Let's go get some coffee, Valerie."

She shudders, puir wee lassie. "This has been a time straight from a nightmare," she says as we make our way through to a small coffee shop in the Hôtel Marquise. I have never been there before. Ellis had always brought me into the room with sofas to have tea.

When we have our coffee, I get straight to the point, because I have no taste for this kind of conversation and I don't want to drag it out.

"How awful for you, Valerie! Being right in the middle of it when those bombers were trying to get hold of a detonator to blow us all to smithereens. You must be terrified."

"Not so terrified as on Friday," she blurts out, and then puts her hands over her mouth as she realises what she's said. "It was so frightening." she adds, almost to herself. "Why did he have to come to Paris? And then Harry said to show him the view. I don't know why Harry even brought him!"

"Harry brought him?"

"Yes, don't you remember? I told you. I was going to the van to get a filled croissant for my supper, and I met Harry coming in!"

She doesn't remember anything clearly. She thinks that she has told me all this before.

So I say, "Harry came in with Ferghal and Charlie Stout?"

But I'm not really asking. My tone is the tone in which I let a girl know that the answer she has given me is correct. Valerie responds to it. She glows just like the girls in 5C do.

Poor Valerie! So desperate for praise, so seldom getting it.

Valerie is continuing. "Harry and I went into the ticket queue. But then Ferghal came. And he said something about wires. I don't remember what, it didn't make sense. But Harry said we would leave the queue because he needs to do what Ferghal wanted.

"And I said that this is not a problem, because I can stay in the queue. What is it that he wants me to say for him to the ticket staff?

"But Harry doesn't tell me. He says, *'No, someone must stay with Charlie Stout, he must be watched.'* And he tells me to take him to the top of the tower. I don't want to.

'Why must he be watched?' I ask. *'Why cannot Ferghal watch him? I did not bring him. I want to go home.'"*

And she breaks down completely and begins to cry.

This is not turning out as I thought. Valerie is not confessing to a murder or even to being involved in an accidental death. She is confessing to being an unwilling accomplice to the bomb plot. Even if she escapes the death sentence for the murder, which she might because the murder wasn't pre-meditated and she was in a terrible state at the time, the French poliss will nab her for terrorism.

I'm not sure that Charlie Stout's death wasn't accidental, after all. But it makes no difference. They will lock her up and throw away the key. She will never come out of this, never.

I'm heart sorry for Valerie. But Lianna's freedom is at stake too, and I harden my heart.

I reach over and stroke her hair. "It's OK," I murmur "It's OK." Knowing that it's anything but OK. My heart is breaking for her. But I go on extracting the confession.

She turns and casts herself into my arms and she's crying as if she will never stop. "It was so awful." she says. "Who would have thought it of Ferghal?"

Thought what? I'm getting confused. But I steel myself to deceive her and go on stroking her hair as I ask, "So Harry made you take Stout up the Tower in the lift?"

She raises her head in astonishment, tears pouring down her face.

"No, of course not. He needs me to translate. It is Ferghal that he sends with my fa… fath…" and she's crying a torrent again.

This story is growing still more tangled, and I'm lost. What happened? Was it Ferghal who threw him from the Tower? But it can't have been.

Valerie was there. I remember her voice on the tape. *I hate you!* click *You should never have come here. You will not go away again. You horrible, wicked, cruel man, you deserve to burn in hell forever.*

The words were recorded at the Tower, she was there with him when she said it. She **must** have thrown him to his death.

Tearfully she gets out her story. They were all together at the top of the Tower. Ferghal. Harry. Valerie. Charlie Stout. The lift attendant, whose name is Henri something.

Ferghal tells everyone – she wasn't coherent enough for me to understand why – that Stout is Valerie's father. He's sneering about the old photo of Charlie Stout Valerie keeps in her car. Valerie is devastated. She stammers out that Ferghal is wrong, but everyone knows (or poor overwrought Valerie thinks they know) her father is standing there refusing to acknowledge her, just as he has always done. She is beyond reason, overcome with shame.

She begins screaming at Stout. *"I hate you! I wish you were dead! You should never have come here. You will not go away again. You horrible, wicked, cruel man, you deserve to burn in hell forever."*

But Tax Charlie just stands there, staring at her without saying anything for a few moments, and then he turns to Harry and begins to speak to him. Valerie can't bear it. All these years, and now she's right in front of him, and he's still behaving as if she doesn't exist.

At that point in her story, she's too shaken to go on. I make her drink a little water and take some breaths. Gradually her breathing gets less raggedy and she goes on.

When Stout had turned away from her, she charged at him and began to shake him. At first, he tried to get free from her grip on his arms.

Then he begins to shake her too. And as they are rocking back and forth, Tax Charlie bumps into Harry, who drops something.

And then Harry – this is the really horrible bit for Valerie, she has a lot of difficulty in forcing the words out – and then Harry, as calmly as if he were lighting another cigarette, just reaches out, pulls her father out of her hands, puts his hands around Stout's neck, and squeezes.

Stout is struggling, but that doesn't do him any good. Harry squeezes harder, and Stout's face goes purple. He's trying to say something, but no one will ever know what, because Harry squeezes harder still, and the words are lost.

Harry puts on more pressure, and Stout suddenly goes limp.

Then Harry takes his hands away, and Stout drops to the floor.

And Harry lights a cigarette, turns and says to Ferghal, "Take the garbage out."

Just as calmly as if he had really been talking about emptying a trashcan and not – and not – Valerie can't speak anymore, she's practically in hysterics.

So, I calm her and soothe her and make her take a few more sips of water, and then I get the rest of her story, inch by inch.

Ferghal moves forward and picks up whatever it was that Harry dropped – Valerie can't tell me what it was, she never saw it – and gives it back to Harry, who puts it into his pocket.

Then Ferghal waves for Henri to come to him. The two of them pick Stout up, and throw him over the waist-high barrier, off the top of the Tower.

And then Harry takes something out of another pocket, and he shows it to her.

It's a mini-recorder. He hits playback. And Valerie hears her hysterical words: *You should never have come here. You will not go away again.*

"Sounds like a death threat to me, Ferghal," Harry says, looking as unconcerned as if he were ordering a cup of coffee. "What do you think?"

"Sounds like it," Ferghal agrees.

Then Harry and Ferghal tell her that she must lie about everything that has happened or they will make sure that she is accused of Stout's murder.

When they play that recording to her, Valerie realises how bad things look for her. She is terrified that a court would believe what they say, that she is the killer.

Yet crazy and mixed-up as it is, I realise that for Valerie the threat of trial for murder is not the worst part. She'd rather face a death sentence than have people know she's a love-child.

Poor Valerie cannot bear the thought of the circumstances of her birth coming into the open – and when she whispers a little about what things were like for her when she was growing up, I can almost understand how she feels.

Raised by those harsh aunts, who condemned and punished her mother for having taken a lover, whose cruelty is part of why the poor woman was driven to her death.

And when her aunts took Valerie in, they rubbed her nose in how good she must be to try to atone for the sin of having been born.

Yes, the church can be cruel to unwed mothers. But not like that! The church doesn't blame the child. And the mother's family are usually kind. Poor Valerie, she has been so unlucky. And then to meet her father in such a way! How deeply she must have hated him.

But as I had always known in my heart, if only I had allowed myself to believe the truth, she is sweet through and through. She could never have killed anyone.

"I should have known better." I castigate myself. "I have been condemning her on the same kind of nothing evidence that Inspector Clermont used against poor Lianna."

As Valerie whispers on, more facts emerge from her tangled story. It becomes clearer with almost every phrase that she knew nothing about the bomb.

Yes, she is prey to pathological hatred of the father who abandoned her, but she was not part of Harry Brown's vicious conspiracy. She is confused and frightened and upset.

It's clear that she was caught up in the rollercoaster of events, just like me and Lianna.

But unlike us, Valerie is only half a victim. She didn't know anything about the bomb, but she knows Harry and Ferghal are cold-blooded murderers – and she let them get away with it. She was coerced and bullied, but she is still an accessory after the fact.

I soothe her and promise that she will be safe. I don't know whether that's true or not, but what else can I say to the poor lassie?

And then I call in Ellis. As always, he has a solution. He says that there is a place just outside Paris where Valerie can get help. A hospital in a beautiful chateau with acres of grounds. The residents rest and enjoy nature and gradually they heal; those who can be healed.

Ellis tells me that most of the residents in that place are healed eventually because the people who get sent there have all been victims of traumatic events. It's what they've been put through that made them a bit crazy. The doctors who work there slowly help them to become balanced again.

It is the best and safest place for Valerie. Soon the men in white coats come to take her away. She seems willing enough to go. This has been a dreadful time for her, and she is ready to hand her life over to anyone who offers her a respite.

I have recorded everything on the machine Ellis had handed me before Valerie and I went into the coffee shop. Paris is safe. Ferghal and Harry have been picked up. The Benson & Hedges butts Harry left beside the bomb will prove he was a terrorist conspirator, and there is a mountain of other evidence. Everything will be shared with Italian Interpol so that the bombing conspirators there can be caught too.

I am glad now that for a little while I was the goat in the clearing. What Ellis said is true – I wasn't staked there to be eaten, and he didn't let the tiger reach me.

"Buck up, old girl, we need to toddle down to the lockup and get your friend out.

Paris at Leisure

Chapter 15 Paris at Leisure

11:45 p.m. Monday, 17th August, 1970

Hôtel Marquis, Rue Greneta, Paris, France

I'm so happy! It's so wonderful to have Lianna back again! Ellis is treating us both to a late supper at his hotel, unbelievably marvellous food as always.

We are going to be spending the night there after all, because the Sûreté have closed down our *pension* completely while they gather physical evidence.

I didn't think that we would have enough money to pay for so much luxury, but we're the guests of the French government until our package tour room is available again – and we are being paid a staggering amount of compensation for the destruction of all our things.

Plus, there's a big reward for helping to catch the bombers. My head reels when I try to work it out, but it's a *lot* of money, more than a whole year's salary! Lianna says it should be even more than that. She has a very good head on her for money stuff, so she's probably right.

Ellis is amused to see that Lianna is so hard-headed. He promises to help us to get all of our financial rights. I think maybe he's laughing at us, but no, he means it.

He's just smiling because, like me, he's relieved that everything worked out so well.

After dinner, Ellis gravely wishes us both a good night's sleep. He says he will be at work long before we're up in the morning, and gives me the telephone number of an office where he can be reached if we need him. I get the feeling that this is his way of saying goodbye.

I'm a little sad about that. Although I have only known him three days, they have been the most hectic, activity-crammed, terrifying, exhausting days of my life – and he was there for me through it all, feeding me and helping me and keeping me safe.

I think of Ellis as a friend.

I'd hoped that he thought of me as a friend. Didn't he say "now that we're friends"? I suppose that was his way of keeping me under surveillance...

We're up with the lark next morning. They serve us a huge *café complet* in our suite. Yes, suite! Me and Lianna have a big bedroom each and we have a sitting room too. I share the joke with Lianna about me eating *café complet* for two on Sunday morning.

We still have three days left to enjoy Paris and we intend to make the most of it.

For the next three days, me and Lianna are going to be racketing about, cramming in all the best sights and buying all the prettiest clothes and eating all the most delicious meals that a ton of money can buy!

The first thing we do is go to the early Mass at the Basilique du Sacré-Cœur. They have early Mass there every day. Lianna is stunned by the feeling of peace and love from all the prayers seeping into the walls. We light candles and say silent prayers of thanksgiving for Lianna's deliverance – and all the lovely money! Then we find an offerings box and make a donation.

After Mass, well! Neither of us has a stitch to wear except what we stand up in, and there's all that money to be spent! We head for Galeries Lafayette first.

It's not exquisite in the Faberge-Egg-style of Galerie des Arcades, but it's an architectural miracle, crammed with the most colourful shops you ever saw! Just not rich girl shops like in Galerie des Arcades.

And Lianna and me, we like nice things but we're not rich girls and we don't want to spend like rich girls, windfall or not!

The shops in Galeries Lafayette are lots more affordable – and even more beautiful in their own Art Deco way. In Glasgow, we're very proud of our Rennie MacIntosh Art Deco, but the dome of stylised stained glass in what they call the *Coupole* at Galeries Lafayette leaves the MacIntosh House standing!

The *Coupole* rises above the top tier of shops in a breath-taking sweep of beautifully molded and enamel-painted metal girding teased into fantastical shapes, yet strong enough to support thousands of stained glass panels made in such beautiful designs that you could spend all day just craning your neck to look up at the glittering glass-rainbows in that dome.

The *Coupole* proper is sort of a cross between a dome and an atrium, with the shops all built on the outer perimeter of a circle. So the entire area below the dome is a gigantic completely open cylinder rising almost to Heaven, with shops on all sides.

Lianna really enjoys shopping in Galeries Lafayette. The shops rise on three brocaded-stone tiers like a Giant's Opera House, each tier full of ever more exquisite shops.

And when we discover that we can have everything we buy delivered to the Hôtel Marquise within hours – in fact all our parcels will be sitting in our suite before we can get back there ourselves! Well, there's no holding Lianna then.

She goes straight to a luggage shop – except it doesn't just sell luggage, it also sells gorgeous handbags with matching gloves and shoes. Well, when I see all those matched sets of gloves and shoes and bags, I almost die! Lianna chooses a gorgeous steamer trunk for herself, dark brown leather with brass fittings. It's really beautiful, but the price beggars belief.

However, as Lianna loses no time in making me understand, buying quality luggage is an economy because it lasts forever – and we have plenty of money to buy the best because we won't need to buy suitcases.

I didn't quite get that at first, but Lianna is very good at explaining anything to do with shopping. She explains that all we need is a steamer trunk each and a small travelling case.

Steamer trunks are much better than suitcases on the train, because they fit neatly under the berths – luxury trains like the Istanbul Express (which we're travelling on) have stowage spaces inside the compartments where the trunk slides in. You can't do that with suitcases, Lianna explains to me. Obviously, she paid a lot more attention than I did to what the lassie at Thomas Cook was showing us about the accommodation on the train!

So I buy an exquisitely glamorous black glossy trunk with a matching small case for myself. It isn't leather like Lianna's, it's made of glossy fibreglass, so beautiful. And perfectly plain black leather court shoes, with a matching bag and gloves, and an umbrella made of a glossy black shiny material and shaped like a parasol.

I never saw anything so beautiful for keeping off the rain in my life. As Lianna points out, I'll get my money's worth out of that lot when I go back to Glasgow, because these rainy day accessories will last forever and will always look wonderful with any outfit. I also got some lovely black brogues, and a brown pair too.

I don't quite understand why it costs so much to get things that don't have trims and fancy stuff, but Lianna explains it to me. If it's plain, then the leather has to be perfect quality, with no spots or flaws, because there's nothing in the design to cover up any imperfections. I don't really mind the cost, because as Lianna says, over the years I'll get my money's worth – or should I say the French justice system's money's worth – of use out of these lovely things.

Then Lianna decided that we also needed a hat box each, and they have matching hat boxes, too. It's sheer heaven! And then we go shopping for hats. We have to have at least one hat to wear for church on Sundays, naturally, but I am not going to attempt to describe the Parisian hats. The most beautiful things you ever saw! I bought four!

By the time we're ready to begin buying ordinary clothes, I'm starving and my feet hurt.

And we want to make the most of our time and see all the sights we can, so we get a taxi to the Musée de l'Orangerie. In two minutes, we're sitting in the wee restaurant there, looking out at the Place de la Concord with a super view of the lovely fountains while we eat tasting plates. I don't know how anyone is supposed to choose and eat a main dish after eating those lovely bites. Snacking on the tiny morsels becomes the biggest lunch I've ever eaten.

After lunch, we spend an hour looking at the famous art in the museum. Later on, it's hard to choose whether to do more shopping or go sightseeing. We do need an awful lot of clothes, and night things and toiletries and all sorts...

But there are so many wonderful sights to see as well!

Lianna finds the perfect compromise. We go to the Musée du Parfum Fragonard, which is a behind-the-scenes tour of Fragonard perfumes. Le Musée du Parfum is a lovely old building that has an incredible collection of perfume bottles and perfume-making devices, some very ancient. We spend a delightful hour pottering about, and then Lianna takes charge of getting all of the stuff for making us pretty and sweet-smelling.

She asks me to choose which scent I like best, and then she buys the most stylish range of toiletries like you cannot imagine! Every last one of them in an exquisite glass bottle, each bottle different. I'm staggered at the price, but this time Lianna doesn't even bother to explain to me why it's more economical to buy all this mind-blowingly expensive stuff.

She just says we deserve a treat, after all we've been through.

After that, we go back to Galeries Lafayette and shop until we drop.

At dinnertime, we're going for a cruise on the Seine. We have a lovely table by the window, and see all the sights as the boat floats down the river, like the Louvre, Ile de la Cité, and the Gare d'Orsay. By the time they've welcomed and seated us, the buildings are all lit up and they look wonderful against the night sky.

They give us a glass of champagne when we board. Lianna has mine as well as her own, and doesn't complain when I say that's enough wine for one evening. She's too busy enjoying the live music. Although she does have a couple of glasses of wine later, with the meal, and I join her in a glass then. Who can say *No* to French wine?

When the boat docks, we're more than happy to walk back to the Hôtel Marquis and sink into our lovely comfy beds...

N ext day we devote to serious shopping – we can't turn up in Istanbul with no clothes – although we do make time to visit Le Petit Trianon, the wee summer palace at Versailles where Marie Antoinette used to play at being a farm girl.

If she'd ever seen what a real farm's like, well, she wouldn't have liked it, that's all I'm saying. But it was a lovely tour. The buildings are very elegant, and they took us around in a special touring car, which was a nice rest for feet aching from going around the shops.

After the Trianon, Lianna and me both feel that's enough sightseeing for one day, and we go back to the hotel for a nice quiet dinner and a good rest. I sort of hope Ellis will be there, but we don't see him.

O ur last day! Over breakfast we decide that we'll visit Sainte-Chapelle and the Louvre – how could we hold our heads up back home, when we tell them we've been to Paris, and they speir about the Mona Lisa, and we have to tell them we didn't see it! For sure, we have to visit the Louvre. But I don't much fancy a lot of walking, so we'll just spend a couple of hours there. And then do a little last-minute shopping, and spend the evening at a cabaret.

Ultimate luxury and decadence, here we come!

When we finish our breakfast and go downstairs, we discover that the Sûreté have finished collecting evidence and so we should be moving back into our *pension* now.

But we have a mountain of shopping sitting in our rooms, and we don't fancy having to haul it along to Hôtel Albert. Besides, this is our last day in Paris. We don't want to waste hours of it messing about changing hotels. So we make up our minds to be madly extravagant, and we spend our own money on paying to stay in our lovely suite for one last night.

I do not even want to think about what it costs. But as Lianna says, it's coming out of our reward money for helping to catch the bombers, so the French government is really paying for us anyway; it's just the same as if we were still their guests.

We spent most of our damage compensation money on buying all our wonderful new things, but we haven't touched our reward money yet. So Lianna is right as usual. What a head that lassie has on her for dealing with money!

We're boarding the train for Istanbul today. Our journey across Europe starts at 10:35 a.m. We're standing on the platform, and I'm zealously watching the porters' every movement as they stow our new luggage in our compartment. I don't want to take any risk that our lovely travel things might get damaged by careless handling.

I'm checking our tickets again to make certain sure that we have the right compartment when Ellis comes up to us.

"Good morning, Major," says Lianna, likely because she doesn't feel that she knows him well enough to call him anything else. She's only spent one evening in his company. And he's so much older than us. Lianna was brought up right, like me. She's respectful to her elders.

With a tiny half-bow, Ellis hands her a small bundle of books. "To keep you busy on the journey." He grins. Lianna blushes. I blush.

Then he turns to me and hands me a cake box. "To make up for the cream cakes you didn't get on the train from Le Havre."

My face gets redder. "It's very kind of you to come to see us off."

But he interrupts, "Oh, I'm not seeing you off. I'm travelling to Rome. Time to get aboard, ladies."

He tips his hat to us and saunters off to the First Class section of the train.

For the first time, I regret not having spent the extra money for First Class. Lianna and I are standing right beside our own Second Class compartment, and we climb aboard.

I wonder what adventures await us in Istanbul? It's bound to feel tame after all the ups and downs we've had in Paris.

The guard blows his whistle and we're off.

As Lianna slides open the door of our lovely compartment, made up as a tiny sitting room, a train attendant rushes up. "A million pardons, ladies. This is not your compartment."

I have the tickets still in my hand, and it's our compartment all right. I turn to the man and show him our tickets. "It is so."

He beams. "Yes, ladies. From Rome to Istanbul, this is your compartment. From here to Rome, you have been transferred to a suite in First Class. Please, follow me."

No way am I leaving my exquisite new black luggage to the tender mercies of careless train porters. It will be moved under my eye. "Very well." I sniff. "Please ask the porters to come for our luggage now."

The attendant is crestfallen. Obviously, he thought that we would be overjoyed to get moved into one of the super-ritzy First Class compartments just as fast as possible. He peeps into our compartment. Our tiny travelling cases sit on a teeny-weeny shelf of just the right size to hold them. Lianna is a superb shopper – she knew exactly what we'd need.

The attendant beams again. "Of course. I will carry your cases." He darts in too fast for me to say a word, picks up our cases, and is back out in the passageway with us almost before I've opened my mouth.

"Thank you." I smile. "But we'll still need a porter. There are two steamer trunks as well." The attendant knows all about the compartments where steamer trunks are stowed, of course. It's quickly settled that Lianna will go with him and our travelling cases to our new First Class suite, and I'll wait here for the porters. You couldn't move me with a crowbar before those lovely trunks are safely transported.

Soon two porters turn up. Only one can work inside the compartment at a time. The first goes into the compartment, opens the stowage, carefully removes Lianna's trunk, and starts off down the passageway with it. The other goes to the stowage compartment on the opposite side of the carriage, opens it up, and begins to pull out my gorgeous, glossy black trunk.

Three seconds later he stops dead, and backs out of the carriage, his body obscuring my view. Obviously, my worst fears have been realised – some careless porter has scratched my trunk!

I crane my neck, determined to see the extent of the damage. And when I do, I wish I hadn't. The top of my trunk is not properly closed, and a lifeless arm lolls out of it.

THE END

If you enjoyed this story, please help new readers to find it. Reviews are the breath of life to new books and new Indie authors like me, the way that most readers first find us.

Please share Màiri with the world so that I can keep on writing new adventures for her!

https://amazon.com/review/create-review?&asin=B09PMP4J6Y

A Few Words from Kate

Hello there. Thank you for reading *Death in Paris*. I hope that you enjoyed it. I wrote this little book to help people escape from the worries of COVID and political tension into a better world, if only for a couple of hours.

The better world in these pages isn't a fantasy, it really existed back in 1970. The people in that world - and it's the people who make it a place worth visiting - really existed then too. Glasgow was full of women like Kat and Morag and Màiri and Lianna. I hope that you enjoyed meeting them in these pages and that you'll come back to Kat's kitchen often, for a cup of tea and a bit of a *craic*.

Morag's Cookbook will be coming out in June or July 2022, and Maryna, one of my many friends in the Ukraine, is making a video to show you exactly how to bake Brandy Snaps. Yum!!

I'm happy to say that Maryna and her family are safe and well.

The world was in a bit of a mess back in 1970 too. It was the Time of The Troubles, and life wasn't a picnic! By 1972/3 ordinary people's lives were under constant threat in Britain due to IRA bombing. And yet the IRA were Freedom Fighters, they were doing their best (in the wrong way, of course) to bring into the Court of World Opinion the relentless religious persecution in the British-ruled Ireland of the time.

When Màiri speaks of the English authorities of her time as Imperialists and oppressors, she is speaking of literal fact. But I'm not on a soapbox here. I want you all to have a good laugh, because Laughter Is The Best Medicine. We all need some Good Medicine in these difficult times. I hope that you laughed at least once while reading Màiri's adventures.

How long will this series last? From July 1970 to Christmas 1975. By then the world was a different place. I hope to write a new Màiri mystery every 6 weeks for the rest of 2022, and I might manage it, because she's a real person to me, and "fictional real people" tend to write themselves - because they've got something to say. Wish me luck!

Speaking of luck, Màiri's had a lot. Not only did she survive all her peril in these pages; not only did she meet Ellis Peverel, a true friend to her - and a man so unlike Brian that we hope (at least I do) they will become more than friends; but the real world has been kind to her.

Death in Paris was released on 30th March 2022. Today is 5th May 2022, and *Death in Paris* has already won a major award - The Independent Publisher Book Awards Bronze Medal for Best Mystery & Suspense eBook - an IPPY.

More importantly, at least to me, in the last 5 weeks over 250 reader reviews have been posted across the internet. I am thrilled that so many of you took the time to write and tell me - and the world - that you enjoyed being with our girls for a few hours.

The sad fact is, that lots of people can't afford to buy books right now. That's Life In The Time Of COVID. I'm doing what little lies in my power to help.

Death in Paris the eBook has been downloaded for free over 9,000 times.

Morag's Cookbook eBook is free to all my readers. If you can't find a free copy, then email me asking for one. *Màiri Meets Khrushchev* will be free to all my readers as soon as it's ready for release. I want you all to enjoy our girl's adventures without worrying about money.

But I have to eat too, so I can't make **every** *Màiri* book free. If you had a light-hearted moment reading this book, then do please try to help your financially challenged friends get a little sparkle into their day, by asking your local library to stock Màiri's mysteries. Librarians **like** it when people ask them to stock a book.

My local library will stock the *Màiri* paperbacks, and yours could too. A Large Print version is available. And soon an Audiobook will be ready too.

Email me anytime. I love getting your thoughts on Màiri's Life and Times—and what you say **does** influence what I write.

Kate Darroch, Ilfracombe, Devon. 5th May 2022.
email: kate@katedarroch.com

See my blog on Goodreads for a daily laugh!
https://www.goodreads.com/author/show/22133773.Kate_Darroch/blog

If you have enjoyed *Death in Paris* and you would like to read more of my books then please help me to spend more time writing! I spend 3 hours publicising my work for every hour that I write. Please help me to turn those numbers upside down by sharing your joy ☺
I enjoyed *Death in Paris* and I'd like to review
https://amazon.com/review/create-review?&asin=B09PMP4J6Y

Acknowledgements

Thank you my darling Matt, whose love and kindness and generosity make so many things possible that would otherwise be out of reach.

Thank you my dear friend Andrew, whose practical help and support made it possible for me to become an Indie publisher.

Thank you my loving sister Helen, for the example of your successful Romance books.

Thank you my thoughtful brother Robert, for thinking every day about how to support my efforts.

Thank you my loving brother Lucius, for keeping me grounded.

Thank you my brilliant Marcus, for encouraging me to work on despite my ill health.

Thank you my sainted ever-beloved mother, whose example taught me to ignore the cruelty of nay-sayers.

Thank you author Susan Gast, whose kindness to me knows no bounds.

Thank you Jerri Cachero, who does so much for fledgling Cozy authors, for your generosity and for Hosting my Launch Party. Jerri, may God send you health. Sending healing energy with love. You are in my prayers.

Thank you Cozy author Sabetha Danes, who does so much for fellow Cozy authors, for your help and support which made my Launch so much easier, and generously recommending *Death in Paris* to your readers. Sabetha, your family are in my prayers at this very difficult time for you.

Thank you Cozy author Lynn Morrison, who has been such a good friend to my writing, for your help and support which made my Launch Party a joy! And for generously recommending *Death in Paris* to your readers.

Thank you Cozy author Jennifer Alderson, for coming to my Launch Party and so generously recommending *Death in Paris* to your readers.

Thank you Cozy author Amy Vansant, who does so much for Indie authors everywhere, for your help and support which made my Launch much easier, and for generously recommending *Death in Paris* to your readers.

Thank you Cozy author Anne Shillolo, for generously recommending *Death in Paris* to your readers, and for pledging your support for my future books!

Thank you Cozy author Paul James, for rallying appreciation for *Death in Paris* in Canada, and for generously recommending *Death in Paris* to your readers.

Thank you Cozy author Sharon Buck, for encouragement and good advice, and generously recommending *Death in Paris* to your readers.

Thank you Mystery author and teacher Zara Altair, for your help and support.

Thank you author and journalist Frank Daley, for befriending me and giving *Death in Paris* a lovely write up.

Thank you my friend Deb, who does not wish to take credit, for so kindly and generously taking time out from your own work to create all the truly gorgeous Chapter illustrations for my books!

Thank you Matt Stone, Chariz, and Carin, for working tirelessly to make possible all the wonderful graphics for *Death in Paris*

Thank you Sandy Beckwith, whose multiple award winning blog Build Book Buzz contains so much which is helpful; and who has been so generous with her time.

Thank you author Laurence O'Bryan, and all your team, for supporting me with incredibly helpful introductions.

Thank you Nick and Cary and Lise and Fiona and Craig and Jamie and Evan and Monica and Kelly and Heather for your help publicising *Death in Paris*

Thank you Dave Chesson for making opaque book marketing tech much easier to understand

A Special Thank You to author David Gaughran for the incredible generosity with which you provide a colossal amount of information to fledgling authors 100% free, and with no thought but to help.

A big thank you to the lovely team at my local library, who have been so kind and helpful in so many ways.

A Thousand Thanks to the many, many ARC readers and eReaders of the *Death in Paris* eBook edition who generously took the time to review my mystery!

and finally -

A HUGE THANK YOU to my darling Beta Readers, to whom this book is dedicated. You taught me so much.

Susan Gast; Madhuparna Goswami; Sharon Hopwood; Christine Kelly; Jenn Olsen; Amy Stone; Tanya Gates; Melanie Di Brizzi; Subhadra Harish; Danette Fowlie; Hilary Walker.

Death
on the Istanbul Express

Death on the Istanbul Express

Chapter One FORTY MINUTES EARLIER

10:00 a.m. Friday, 21st August 1970

Holding cell, Commissariat De Police Quartier De La Porte Saint-Denis

Rue de Chabrol, Paris

The moment has come. Either Harry's cronies will come through for them, or they will spend the rest of their lives rotting at the bottom of the deep hole the French authorities will throw them into. Captured would-be bombers are not popular people, and the Sûreté are especially unhappy with Harry Brown and his soi-disant OAS army because they had come so close to succeeding.

If not for that imbecile Ferghal, Harry thinks – not for the first time – Paris would be in ruins by now. It had been such a brilliant plan. Getting himself onto the committee for the Bastille Day celebrations, throwing money and fancy dinners around like confetti, gradually creating an environment where the staff at the Eiffel Tower *expected* him to turn up at all sorts of odd hours burdened with heavy electronic equipment and ready to start wiring up fireworks.

He'd given them the most spectacular pyrotechnics display they'd ever had, this July 14th.

And if not for that infuriating little Glaswegian school teacher, on August 19th he'd have given them the most terrifying display they'd ever had.

They'd all have been blown to bits, and he would be on his way, this very minute, to his tropical island, a whole island all his own.

Instead he's sitting in an airless room concentrating on not biting his nails. A true leader, (Harry soothes himself with his favourite mantra) a true leader always acts, he does not permit himself to be acted upon by untoward circumstance.

The rescue team will turn up, because they need him. He's got more brains in his little finger that all the rest of them put together have got in their heads. Besides, he's the only one who knows where the weapons are cached.

Harry hasn't been permitted to keep his watch, of course, but his internal body-clock tells him it's close to ten o'clock. They are due to be moved at 10:15 a.m. so at any moment now the guards will be coming to take them to the police transport. Ferghal flexes his biceps and tenses, readying himself to attack.

"Not now, you moron." Harry snarls.

"Sorry, boss."

The gendarmes may arrive at any moment, now is not the time to walk Ferghal through the plan again. But since the idiot could ruin everything by attacking as soon as the police escort walk in, Harry decides that another rehearsal is the lesser danger.

"Listen up Ferghal. Very soon the police will come for us."

"Yes, boss."

" – and when they do, they'll find us sitting here quietly."

"I'll be doing my Zen meditation." Ferghal nods.

"NO Ferghal, not yet."

"But boss - "

"You'll be doing your Zen meditation as we're walking to the transport."

Ferghal manages to look both rebellious and quelled at the same time, and opens his mouth.

Seeing instantly that the word about to issue from him is Not Yes, Harry moves slightly to gain maximum leverage and swings one hand-cuffed wrist into Ferghal's face. The iron cuff doesn't quite reach the moron's mouth, but at least he abandons the attempt to speak.

"You'll go into trance as we reach the van – "

Ferghal opens his mouth again, but nervously eyeing Harry's hands, he thinks better of saying what he is about to say; and Harry continues

" – falling into the van as they open the doors. Which will worry them, and then while they're distracted by your motionless body, Rico and his lads will descend, and we'll be offski."

"I thought it was Gilberto coming for us?"

As it happens he's right, and this annoys Harry even more. "Gilberto, Umberto, Renato, Ricardo, who cares?"

"You do, boss."

Impervious to Harry's glare but swift to dodge his moving hands, Ferghal continues placidly

"You don't want Umberto, he's a lousy driver."

10:11 a.m. Friday, 21st August 1970
Lucky 8 Casino, Rue du Faubourg Saint-Denis, Paris

Gilberto is feeling resentful, and in his open-hearted Italian way he is making his feelings known to Rico, nominally his *capo* in this opera-tion. For a start, Gilberto resents that Rico is *capo* in this operation. He, Gilberto, has seniority. Perhaps only 5 weeks, but still, seniority.

He, Gilberto, is the Getaway driver, the most important role in the operation. Is there a better Getaway driver anywhere in Italy? Any-where in Paris? Anywhere – Gilberto waves both his hands expansively on the face of God's beautiful creation? (Gilberto crosses himself.)

There is not. Rico must know there is not.

Rico, keen for Gilberto to talk himself out and get on with the job, nods vigorously. This has the twin advantages of not interrupting Gilberto's flow of speech and being open to more than one interpretation.

Eventually Gilberto gets to his point, which is that he doesn't see why his priceless talents, his unparalleled driving skills, are being wasted on an incompetent Englishman who has been so foolish as to get himself arrested; or why he, Gilberto, is in Paris at all, a city he detests. He wants to be back in Milan, a city he should never have left.

Rico uncrosses his legs, and re-crosses them the other way, waiting to see if Gilberto has finished. Thankfully, he is talked out, for the moment. Now Rico interjects gently that Harry is the only one who knows where the weapons are.

Gilberto, who is not stupid, only too talkative, gets the point. Where are they rendezvousing with Harry after the jailbreak? In Rome, in St Peter's Square, two days from now.

Gilberto is satisfied. They need the weapons, and two days is not long to wait. To wait a shorter while would be foolish, would draw attention. He glances at his watch. 10:14 a.m. Time to get behind the wheel.

As Gilberto leaves, moving smoothly but at high speed, Rico smiles. 45 seconds left, if that, for Gilberto to get from the Lucky 8 to the Secure area at Rue de Chabrol. Since Rico had the foresight to send the heavies to sit in the car 5 minutes ago, there's no question that Gilberto will make it with seconds to spare. He talks too much, but he drives like God's Vengeance.

10:14 a.m. Friday, 21st August 1970

Secure Vehicles area, 43 Rue de Chabrol, behind Commissariat De Police Quartier De La Porte Saint-Denis, Paris

Just as Harry had anticipated, four gendarmes enter the holding room soon after he finishes talking. They form a square around him and Ferghal, shepherd them out of the room, and bring them into the secure vehicles area where the police transport waits.

From that moment onwards, things fail to go according to plan.

They cross the yard and reach the van. Ferghal doesn't go into a trance. He stands beside the transport vehicle looking perfectly normal, putting one foot on the step as if to enter the van. There's no sign of the Getaway car.

Harry wants to kill Ferghal and his Italian fellow conspirators too! But he always stays cool in an emergency. He kicks out at Ferghal's kneecap, sending him writhing to the ground. That will at least create a distraction, Harry reasons, and give him a moment to think.

Two of the police escort seize Harry's arms. Ferghal is kicking about, and one flailing foot catches Harry on the shin, as painfully as if aimed there on purpose. Harry momentarily loses his hold on his temper and kicks Ferghal back.

Gilberto crashes through the locked gates in a Mercedes Estate that has got to be armour plated to have barrelled in like that. He pulls up scant inches away from the police guards.

Gilberto doesn't only drive like the Vengeance of God, he has Zero Tolerance for anything which interferes with his driving. Gilberto is not happy to see Ferghal, who's meant to be in a trance, flopping about on the ground.

He flies out of the car, Peppe and Carlo exiting just behind him.

Scooping up Ferghal with one hand, Gilberto tosses him to Peppe, and Ferghal goes limp in mid-flight, the Zen trance cutting in at the most inconvenient moment possible.

Peppe's out of the fight now, it's going to take all his energy to get this sack of lard into the back seat of the Mercedes.

Peppe calls aloud on the Mother of Mercy for aid. He manages to absorb the dead weight of Ferghal landing in his gorilla-muscled arms, turns swiftly back to the car.

Without even checking his stride, Gilberto barrels on. He plunges both hands into his pockets and brings them out again all in one lightning arc of fluid movement.

At the top of the arc, Gilberto punches the gendarme turning toward him in the stomach.

The gendarme cries out in pain. Gilberto pushes what he's holding straight into the man's opening mouth, his other hand clapped over the gendarme's nose.

Harry is furious. Screaming police were no part of the plan. The noise may bring help. His escape is coming apart. Swiftly Harry brings up his cuffed hands at the best angle to knock out one of the policemen trying to keep hold of his arms. Harry turns, his rising steel-cuffed wrist hitting the other.

Carlo reaches gendarme #4. Like Gilberto, he punches the man and pushes one chloroform pad into his mouth and the other over his nose. Gendarme #4 sinks to the ground.

Carlo grabs Harry and pulls him away from the falling gendarmes who were holding him.

At the same moment, Gilberto seizes Harry around the waist and half carries, half pushes him the two feet to the open back door of the Mercedes.

Harry is bundled into the back seat beside Peppe and Ferghal.

Carlo follows as Gilberto reaches the open driver's door.

Peppe whips out a lockpick.

The car takes off. Back through the crushed gates.

Left into Rue de Chabrol.

Swinging violently right into Rue La Fayette.

Zig zags through the roundabout.

The Mercedes tears on up Rue La Fayette, weaving between the other cars as if they aren't there.

Peppe is releasing Harry from his handcuffs as the car arrows onward.

Carlo unlocks the handcuffs from the wrists of the motionless Ferghal.

As the Mercedes passes Gare du Nord Harry and Ferghal are pushed out of the massively slowed but still moving car. Peppe crams a package into Harry's arms as he tumbles out. Ferghal falls out behind him.

The Mercedes picks up speed, moving on. It vanishes into the traffic stream as if it had never existed.

The entire jailbreak has taken less than 90 seconds.

The Paris police do not even know yet that Harry and Ferghal have escaped.

Now Read On
https://www.amazon.com/gp/product/B09X94SQC7

Titles in Print
Death in Paris
Winner of the Independent Publisher Book Awards Bronze Medal for
Best Mystery & Suspense eBook
Recommended by 26 Cozy Series Authors in the 5 weeks since release *and counting!*
Death on the Istanbul Express

Forthcoming
Death in Rome
Death in Istanbul
They Call Him Gimlet: Major Peverel's Ops
See Kate Darroch's book news at
https://amazon.com/author/kate-darroch
https://KateDarroch.com

If you have enjoyed Death in Paris, then please share the fun
with the world. Reviews help readers to find books they enjoy, and they are the breath of life for new books and new
Indie authors like me.

If you would like to read more of my books then please help
me to spend more time writing! I spend 3 hours publicising
my work for every hour that I write. Please help me to turn
those numbers upside down by sharing your joy ☺
https://amazon.com/review/create-review?&asin=B09PMP4J6Y

Printed in Great Britain
by Amazon

82506254R00115